D1760756

TALES OF THE CLUB EXPERT

TALES OF THE CLUB EXPERT

Jimmy Tait

faber and faber

LONDON · BOSTON

First published in 1987 by
Faber and Faber Limited
3 Queen Square London WC1N 3AU

Typeset by Goodfellow & Egan Cambridge
Printed in Great Britain by
Richard Clay Ltd
Bungay Suffolk
All rights reserved

British Library Cataloguing in Publication Data

Tait, Jimmy
Tales of the club expert.
1. Contract bridge
I. Title
795.41′5′0924   GV1282.3
ISBN 0–571–14870–0

CONTENTS

PREFACE

I've always been a great one for bridge clubs. The first I ever played at on a regular basis was the old Studio Bridge Club at the top end of Queensway, Bayswater. That was in the 1950s. Open seven days a week, the club was manna from heaven to the numerous addicts who found their way to the rickety wooden staircase guarding its doors. Inside it was light and spacious and catered for 3d., 6d. and 1s. players of all shapes and sizes. Alas, the Studio is no longer with us. A victim of redevelopment, it has long since been laid to rest beneath a towering cluster of luxury flats.

In those days there were several other bridge clubs in that area. There was the Grand Slam in Craven Hill Gardens, the Peter Pan in Lancaster Gate and, of course, the Pem Bridge Club in Pembridge Villas, Notting Hill Gate. I passed that way a few days ago and there was still a board outside advertising its presence, though I know for a fact that there hasn't been a game of bridge played there for at least twenty years.

In the 1950s, if you knew where to go, there were several other places in that area where you could always get a game. In Bayswater Road itself, just round the corner from where the Studio used to be, stands the Coburg Hotel. Bridge players were always welcome in the first-floor lounge. One particular female used to gather round her a coterie of bridge players, like a hen with a brood of chicks, and move them around from hotel to hotel in a manner reminiscent of Nathan Detroit's floating crap game.

Not too far away from the clubs I've named stood

another – though I didn't play there in those days. In fact, I didn't even know it existed until a few years ago and yet it seems to have turned out to be the sole survivor. Someone told me that it started life as a small guest-house and was owned by a retired civil servant who was a bridge enthusiast. He didn't get enough guests to make a go of it as a hotel so he converted it into a bridge club instead. He's been dead for years now, but his son has taken over. He's not the player his father was, but doesn't mind the income that the game generates. I'm not going to reveal this club's where-abouts because most of the original members are getting on a bit now and would have a couple of haemorrhages apiece if they suspected their insularity was about to be disturbed by a horde of strangers. All right. Xenophobic if you insist, but that's the way it is. Some people are like that.

I was taken there one rainy afternoon by a friend who thought I might find the place amusing. As we stood in the entrance to the main card-room where two or three tables were already in play, his voice dropped to a reverent whisper. 'Do you see that chap over there?' he said. 'That table on the right – the one in the dark suit? He's our best player. That's the club expert.'

I glanced in the direction he indicated and saw a be-spectacled individual glowering at his partner with ill-concealed displeasure. From that distance I couldn't catch what he was saying, but it looked far from complimentary. An old-fashioned wing collar encased his neck and I caught a glimpse of pink scalp gleaming through short iron-grey hair. On a small table by his side a forgotten cigar smoked in a huge ashtray.

Later on I got to know his name, of course, but he'd be extremely irritated if I let it slip out. For one thing he's rather sensitive about personal matters and for another he knows I'd probably get the spelling wrong. His grand-parents were Eastern European, you see, and most of the

2

members here can't cope with his family name. That doesn't please him either. I suppose that's why they generally refer to him as the club expert. That does!

Anyway, this book is about him and some of the bridge hands with which he has been involved. Over the years I've grown to respect him a great deal. He's certainly the best card player I've ever met and he's taught me more about bridge than I thought possible. I'm hoping he's going to do the same for you.

J.W.T

1

A tale of two minors

The club expert is not an ungenerous man and will usually allow himself to be bought a drink and listen to some bridge problem. Most of the younger members ceased to avail themselves of this facility when it was discovered that his knowledge of bidding theory was virtually non-existent. His methods were to discover as much as possible about his partner's hand while at the same time disclosing to his three adversaries the minimum of information about his own. He had no time at all for modern conventions. 'Transfer bids,' he would say, 'are for footballers not bridge players.' It was one of his favourite maxims.

His strength lay in his assured technique as a card player, and his powers of analysis were remarkable. He was able to pick out the best percentage play from a tangle of red herrings, usually with indecent haste. He was seldom wrong. These facets were on display recently when the youngest member button-holed him with a question about splinters. 'Consult your local timber merchant,' he was told. Undeterred, the youngster produced the following hand which he had played recently in a contract of 6 ♠ – failing by one trick.

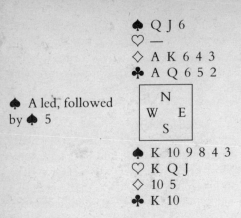

♠ Q J 6
♡ —
♢ A K 6 4 3
♣ A Q 6 5 2

♠ A led, followed by ♣ 5

♠ K 10 9 8 4 3
♡ K Q J
♢ 10 5
♣ K 10

The club expert showed no interest in the bidding after being informed that neither opponent had entered the auction. 'Opening lead?' he snapped. 'Ace and another spade,' he was told, 'East following suit twice.'

The club expert studied the hand for a full five seconds. 'And what's the problem, may I ask?'

'I was wondering whether I should have taken the ruffing finesse.'

'On hands like this ruffing finesses are for children,' said the club expert in a tone that brooked no argument. 'I play for either one of the minor suits to divide no worse than 4–2 and in this eventuality I make the contract with ridiculous ease.'

'But one of the minors *was* 4–2 and I still went down,' persisted the enquirer.

'Then I regret to say you misplayed the hand,' said the club expert. 'Next please.'

How should the slam have been played?

Solution

The declarer should play on diamonds first. If this suit divides no worse than 4–2 the declarer can dispose of a heart loser. Of the other two losers, one can be ruffed and the other goes on the ♣ Q.

If the declarer tries clubs first and encounters a 5–1 break it is too late to turn his attention to diamonds. Insufficient entries make it impossible to set up and enjoy a diamond winner.

Complete deal

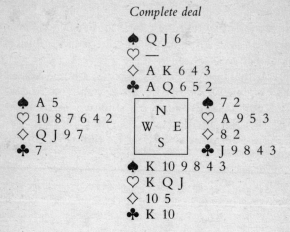

```
              ♠ Q J 6
              ♡ —
              ◇ A K 6 4 3
              ♣ A Q 6 5 2
♠ A 5                         ♠ 7 2
♡ 10 8 7 6 4 2      N         ♡ A 9 5 3
◇ Q J 9 7       W     E       ◇ 8 2
♣ 7                 S         ♣ J 9 8 4 3
              ♠ K 10 9 8 4 3
              ♡ K Q J
              ◇ 10 5
              ♣ K 10
```

2

Give us a break

'Why do they always find these brilliant defences against *me*?' I moaned, wandering into the bridge-club bar during the interval between sessions.

'What is it this time?' someone asked in a bored voice.

'That's extremely kind of you. I'll have a pint. And in return for your generosity allow me to show you this hand I played earlier this afternoon.'

Reaching for an unused beer-mat I scribbled down the following.

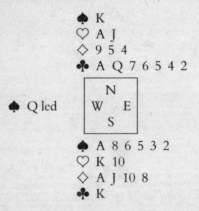

♠ K
♥ A J
♦ 9 5 4
♣ A Q 7 6 5 4 2

♠ Q led

N
W E
S

♠ A 8 6 5 3 2
♥ K 10
♦ A J 10 8
♣ K

'Watch this,' I said. 'The bidding's not important, but you end up in 3 NT and West leads the ♠ Q. You win in dummy and East throws a low heart. You come to hand with the ♣ K and both opponents follow, though West's card is the ♣ 10. This looks ominous, doesn't it? It's then that you have the brilliant idea of using the ♥ J as an extra entry into dummy in case the clubs are 4–1. You can stand the ♡ Q being wrong if the clubs behave, but it gives you can extra chance if they don't. Get it? So you lead the ♡ 10 intending to play dummy's ♡ J. Unfortunately West covers with the ♡ Q – he doesn't know what he's doing of course – the clubs don't break and you end up one down. That's how I played.'

Afterwards I asked West why he'd played the ♡ Q on my ♡ 10.

'Cover an honour with an honour,' he said. 'Marvellous isn't it? If I'd been dealt a small heart instead of the ♡ 10 I'd have made eleven tricks. Talk about being unlucky. I'm seriously thinking about giving up the game.'

My confidant made suitable clucking noises and started to tell me about some foul distribution he had recently encountered so I was quite relieved to hear, 'May I see the hand, please?' from the far end of the bar. Hastily excusing myself I found the club expert enjoying his pre-prandial martini. He listened to my tale of woe, studied the beermat and then pronounced judgement.

'I must say I agree with you,' he said.

'About the heart finesse?' I asked. 'I thought you would.'

'About giving up the game,' he said. 'You didn't give yourself the best chance.'

What had the club expert seen?

Solution

The declarer should play the ♣ A at trick 2 followed by the ♣ Q. If the suit divides 3–2 he is in no difficulty and comes to eleven tricks. If the clubs divide 4–1 he should turn his attention to diamonds, aiming for three tricks in that suit. His first play should be small to the ◇ J (or ◇ 10). If this loses he returns to dummy and leads the ◇ 9. This enables him to pick up the four to an honour in the East hand.

Complete deal

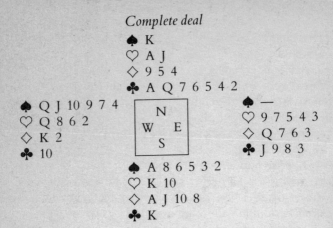

```
                ♠ K
                ♡ A J
                ◇ 9 5 4
                ♣ A Q 7 6 5 4 2
♠ Q J 10 9 7 4       ┌─────────┐       ♠ —
♡ Q 8 6 2            │    N    │       ♡ 9 7 5 4 3
◇ K 2               │ W     E │       ◇ Q 7 6 3
♣ 10                │    S    │       ♣ J 9 8 3
                    └─────────┘
                ♠ A 8 6 5 3 2
                ♡ K 10
                ◇ A J 10 8
                ♣ K
```

3

The club expert tries teams

'Plus 100,' I said nonchalantly.

'And 620,' replied the club expert, puffing on his cigar. 'That's 12 in.'

I looked at him quizzically. For someone who never played duplicate and only with extreme reluctance had agreed to play in a league match because there was no rubber bridge that evening, he was doing all right.

He returned my glance. 'You did well to find an opening spade lead on the hand,' he said. 'Didn't your partner make a bid?'

'He bid clubs,' I replied. 'And that's what I led. But I switched to spades when I got in and that proved good enough. I can't see how you managed to make the contract,' I concluded lamely.

This was the hand in question.

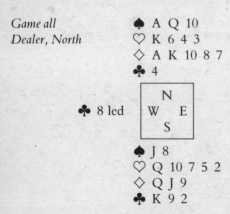

Game all
Dealer, North

♠ A Q 10
♡ K 6 4 3
♢ A K 10 8 7
♣ 4

♣ 8 led

♠ J 8
♡ Q 10 7 5 2
♢ Q J 9
♣ K 9 2

West	North	East	South
	1◇	2♣	2♡
No bid	4♡	All pass	

The bidding was the same at both tables as was the play to the first three tricks which was as follows:

	West	North	East	South
Trick 1	8♣	4♣	A♣	2♣
Trick 2	3♣	10♠	Q♣	K♣
Trick 3	9♡	K♡	8♡	2♡

At this stage each declarer followed a different line. The club expert went on to make the contract while his opposite number failed. What is the correct line of play?

Solution

At trick 4 the declarer should lead diamonds. West ruffs the third round and switches to a spade. Declarer rises with the ♠ A and leads the fourth diamond discarding his remaining spade. The contract is made for the loss of two trumps and a club.

If at trick 4 the declarer continues hearts, West (with ♡ A J) wins and switches to a spade. It is too late now for the declarer to play on diamonds as West can ruff the third round and give partner his spade trick.

Complete deal

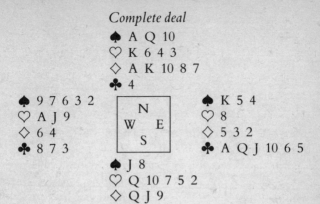

```
                  ♠ A Q 10
                  ♡ K 6 4 3
                  ◇ A K 10 8 7
                  ♣ 4
♠ 9 7 6 3 2      ┌─────────┐      ♠ K 5 4
♡ A J 9          │    N    │      ♡ 8
◇ 6 4            │ W     E │      ◇ 5 3 2
♣ 8 7 3          │    S    │      ♣ A Q J 10 6 5
                 └─────────┘
                  ♠ J 8
                  ♡ Q 10 7 5 2
                  ◇ Q J 9
                  ♣ K 9 2
```

4

Everything was wrong

'One off, partner, I'm afraid. There was nothing I could do. Everything was wrong.'

Grim-faced the club expert listened to the familiar words but made no reply. He had been called away from the table while putting down the dummy hand and had missed the play completely. On his return his partner, endeavouring to make a contract of 6 NT, had already conceded one down and was now dealing the cards for the next hand.

The club expert forced himself to smile. He made it a wide friendly one. 'Couldn't something be done with the club suit?' he asked.

'No chance. They were 5–0 offside. My left-hand opponent held ♣ K 10 8 7 6,' he was told. 'Mind you, I still make the contract if the heart finesse is right. But it wasn't. I was just unlucky.'

'You had five diamonds then?'

His partner looked surprised. 'That's right. Solid, too. I had a 21 count.'

The club expert leaned back happily in his chair. He had enough information now to mentally reconstruct the hand which he visualized as being something like this:

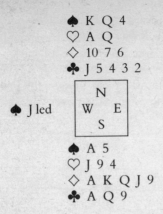

♠ K Q 4
♡ A Q
♢ 10 7 6
♣ J 5 4 3 2

♠ J led

N
W   E
S

♠ A 5
♡ J 9 4
♢ A K Q J 9
♣ A Q 9

Against 6 NT the lead had been the ♠J. He knew that. Now how would his partner have played? It looked natural to win the opening lead in dummy and play a club. When East showed out he would have realized that he could take only two tricks in the suit. He would probably have played the ♣ Q losing to West's ♣ K and would rely on the heart finesse for his contract. Yes that must have been it. He might have played a few rounds of diamonds first, but it would have boiled down to the heart finesse in the end. The ♡ K is offside so the contract goes one down. QED.

He was aroused from his reverie by a sharp voice from across the table. 'Two passes to you, partner.'

'Sorry,' he said, 'I was still thinking about the last hand.'

'Forget it,' he was told. 'Everything was wrong. The contract was unmakeable. Ask anyone. If you had seen my cards you would have known. I guarantee not even you would have made twelve tricks.'

The club expert looked at him. 'Want to bet?' he asked.

How should the contract have been played?

Solution

The declarer is correct in winning the opening lead in dummy and trying clubs at trick 2. When East shows void, however, he should play the ♣ A and at trick 3 lead the ♣ 9 towards dummy's ♣ J. West is unable to play the ♣ K (otherwise the declarer has three club tricks). Declarer wins with dummy's ♣ J and returns to hand with the ♠A to take the heart finesse. Even though this loses, he has twelve tricks and the defence can never come to their club trick.

Complete deal

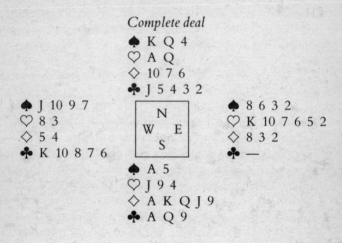

♠ K Q 4
♡ A Q
♢ 10 7 6
♣ J 5 4 3 2

♠ J 10 9 7
♡ 8 3
♢ 5 4
♣ K 10 8 7 6

♠ 8 6 3 2
♡ K 10 7 6 5 2
♢ 8 3 2
♣ —

♠ A 5
♡ J 9 4
♢ A K Q J 9
♣ A Q 9

5

A watched pot

The club expert arrived in the bridge room some twenty minutes later than usual and was annoyed to find only one table in play and no one waiting for a game. He was never at his most comfortable when kibitzing but, on being told that the score was game all, he sat down heavily behind one of the players and waited for the rubber to finish. A watched pot never boils, they say, and several times within the next hour he glanced at his watch with ill-concealed irritation as first one side and then the other squandered chances of administering the *coup de grâce*. Eventually the following hand was dealt and played by one of the participants in 3 NT.

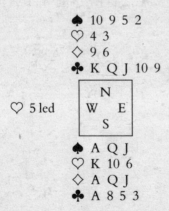

```
            ♠ 10 9 5 2
            ♡ 4 3
            ◇ 9 6
            ♣ K Q J 10 9
                  ┌─────┐
                  │  N  │
  ♡ 5 led        │ W E │
                  │  S  │
                  └─────┘
            ♠ A Q J
            ♡ K 10 6
            ◇ A Q J
            ♣ A 8 5 3
```

The opening lead was the ♡ 5 on which East played the ♡ A and returned the ♡ J. The declarer mismanaged the play with the dual result of further prolonging the rubber and causing the club expert to leave his chair and head in the direction of the snooker room.

'The standard of card playing in this club is definitely getting worse,' he said, deftly potting the pink. 'How the fellow could go down when the opening lead told him that the hearts were no worse than 5–3 beats me. Incidentally, the clubs broke 3–1.'

No one seemed sure of the implication of his closing remark, but how should the contract have been played?

Solution

To avoid having to guess which finesse to take, the declarer should end-play West forcing him to lead into one of the tenaces. This can only be done by exiting with a heart. The declarer should therefore win the ♡ K at trick 2. He must now eliminate West's clubs so three rounds are led ending in hand. At trick 6 declarer exits with the ♡10. West can take tricks 7 and 8 with heart winners, but at trick 9 must lead into one of the declarer's major tenaces. Declarer makes the last five tricks with two club winners, two tricks in the suit led and the ace of the other suit.

Complete deal

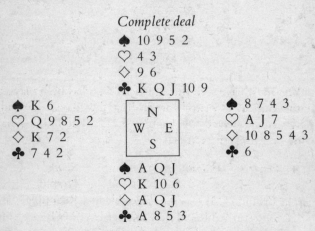

```
              ♠ 10 9 5 2
              ♡ 4 3
              ◇ 9 6
              ♣ K Q J 10 9
♠ K 6                           ♠ 8 7 4 3
♡ Q 9 8 5 2       N             ♡ A J 7
◇ K 7 2        W     E          ◇ 10 8 5 4 3
♣ 7 4 2           S             ♣ 6
              ♠ A Q J
              ♡ K 10 6
              ◇ A Q J
              ♣ A 8 5 3
```

6

The meat in the sandwich

The club expert was not the greatest of socializers so I was quite surprised when he perched himself on an adjoining stool in the bridge-club bar. 'Finish your sandwich,' he said. 'I've a bridge hand to show you.' He helped himself to my serviette and quickly scribbled down the following:

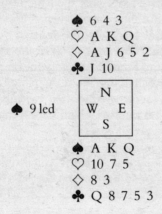

♠ 6 4 3
♡ A K Q
♢ A J 6 5 2
♣ J 10

♠ 9 led

♠ A K Q
♡ 10 7 5
♢ 8 3
♣ Q 8 7 5 3

'You must have seen the American who has been playing in the club as a visitor for the last few days,' he said. 'Anyway, he played this hand in 3 NT. The bidding has some bearing so here it is.'

West	North	East	South
		No bid	No bid
No bid	1♢	Double	Redouble
No bid	No bid	1♠	2 NT
No bid	3 NT	All pass	

'You might conclude from the above auction,' he went on, 'that East has the values of a near opening bid and probably a five-card spade suit.'

Against 3 NT the lead was the ♠ 9 and the declarer led a club at trick 2. East won the ♣ K and continued spades, West following. The declarer led another club to dummy's ♣ J and this held the trick.

'Well! Well! The meat's just fallen from the sandwich,' said the club expert.

'Has it really?' I asked, quickly glancing down at my plate.

'No! No! You misunderstand me,' he replied, a trace of irritation in his voice. 'That's what the American said. It's an expression they use over there when things don't go quite according to plan. Naturally, the declarer would have been better placed if the defence had taken the trick. As it was he was stranded in dummy. Mind you, he recovered well by leading a low diamond from the table. East won with the blank ◇ Q and the American was subsequently able to take a diamond finesse to land his contract.'

'Yes, he's a fair player,' I observed.

'I've seen worse,' conceded the club expert with reluctance, 'but the question I wanted to ask you is this. Do you think that the meat should have been allowed to fall from the sandwich in the first place?'

Solution

For want of a better line of play the declarer is virtually committed to playing on the club suit. However, a more promising line after winning the spade continuation at trick 3 is to cross to dummy with a heart and have the second club lead come from the table. This enables him to overtake in hand if East shows up with ♣ AK9 for example. By overtaking he can also cope with ♣ 9x (West) and ♣ AKxx (East). If the ♣ 9 does not appear on the second round he still has the option of playing for the clubs to be

3–3 or East to hold a singleton diamond honour. Playing the second club from dummy (instead of from his own hand) gives the declarer extra chances.

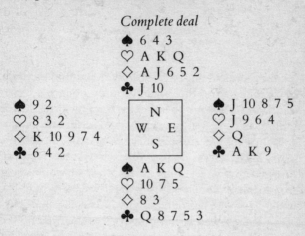

Complete deal

♠ 6 4 3
♡ A K Q
♢ A J 6 5 2
♣ J 10

♠ 9 2
♡ 8 3 2
♢ K 10 9 7 4
♣ 6 4 2

♠ J 10 8 7 5
♡ J 9 6 4
♢ Q
♣ A K 9

♠ A K Q
♡ 10 7 5
♢ 8 3
♣ Q 8 7 5 3

7

The theory of variable opposites

The club expert had no time for modern bidding methods, but he did like to play the weak notrump. Long ago he had realized that, in the right hands, it was a powerful weapon admirably suited to his style. He had no wish, however, to neutralize his chances of becoming declarer by encouraging its use by his partners. He therefore actively discouraged it and insisted that any partner of his must play the strong notrump while accepting that he himself was allowed to play the weak. This was part of his theory of variable oppposites. The arrangement had been in force for some time now to everyone's mutual advantage. There had been 'incidents' in the early days, but once the teething troubles were over the system worked extremely well.

The drawback, of course, was if someone unfamiliar with these methods came to play rubber bridge at the club. This happened only a few days ago when a visitor arrived and cut the club expert in the first rubber of the afternoon session. Smiling pleasantly across the table, he enquired, 'Variable notrump, partner?'

'Certainly,' said the club expert, agreeably surprised to find the stranger conversant with his methods. 'I play the weak notrump and you, of course, will play the strong.'

'You would like to play the strong notrump?' asked the visitor, a puzzled frown on his face.

'No! No!' said the club expert, irritated by the man's presumption. 'It is *you* who will play the strong notrump. I, as befits the stronger player, will use the weak. Surely that's not too difficult for you to understand?'

'What is the system called?' he was asked.

'It is not a system,' explained the club expert testily. 'It is a theory, or at least part of one. It is in fact a major principle of my theory of variable opposites.'

'I'm afraid I have no idea of what that means,' said the stranger apologetically.

'It should be clear enough to a person of the meanest intelligence,' snapped the club expert, rapidly losing his temper, 'but apparently it isn't.' He explained his theory in full.

Ten minutes later, when the theory was fully understood by the visitor, he declined to accept it, so to avoid further strain on his blood pressure the club expert, seething with anger, agreed to play the variable notrump as conventionally practised. Stony-faced he watched in silence as his partner dealt the cards, carefully sorted his hand into suits, and opened 1NT.

Afterwards, he was telling us about it in the bridge-club bar. 'Look at this,' he said, writing down the following hand.

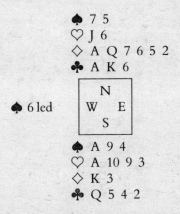

♠ 7 5
♡ J 6
♢ A Q 7 6 5 2
♣ A K 6

♠ 6 led

N
W   E
S

♠ A 9 4
♡ A 10 9 3
♢ K 3
♣ Q 5 4 2

'As South my partner opened 1 NT. With the North hand I had no option but to raise to 3 NT. Naturally, I employed the Stayman Convention *en route* to discourage a major suit lead, but to no avail. West woodenly led the ♠ 6 from a five-card suit and although the declarer held up the ♠ A until the third round, he found the subsequent play too difficult and went one down. The hand is a good example of another principle in my theory of variable opposites since if I had been in his position, I would have made the contract with an overtrick.'

How should the contract have been played?

Solution

The hand is easy unless West turns up with four diamonds. In these circumstances the declarer can only make the contract if East's singleton is the ◇ J. He should cross to dummy with a club at trick 4 and lead a low diamond allowing East to hold the trick if the ◇ J appears.

Complete deal

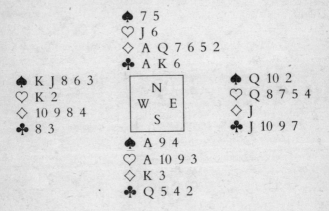

```
              ♠ 7 5
              ♡ J 6
              ◇ A Q 7 6 5 2
              ♣ A K 6
♠ K J 8 6 3                    ♠ Q 10 2
♡ K 2          N               ♡ Q 8 7 5 4
◇ 10 9 8 4   W   E             ◇ J
♣ 8 3          S               ♣ J 10 9 7
              ♠ A 9 4
              ♡ A 10 9 3
              ◇ K 3
              ♣ Q 5 4 2
```

8

Still waters

'In this game,' said the club expert reflectively, 'it is important not to commit yourself unreservedly to one particular line. Moreover,' he went on, 'indecision in the play has also been known to lead to unfortunate results. The secret, of course, lies in good timing as every serious practitioner knows. Patience, too, is a quality which we should all do well to cultivate.'

'I couldn't agree more,' I said. 'We've been here for two hours now and you still haven't had a bite.'

Earlier that day I had accepted the club expert's kind offer to take me for a drive in the country, little knowing that mid-afternoon would find me damp and uncomfortable on a river bank. My companion, installed in the relative comfort of a canvas chair, pensively gazed at his float. So far its equilibrium had remained completely undisturbed.

'Nevertheless,' he continued, unmoved by my outburst, 'Fabian tactics have much to recommend them. The bridge hand I am about to show you is a good illustration of this. If you would kindly pass me your copy of *The Times* I shall try to squeeze it in a vacant margin.'

Writing quickly he produced the following:

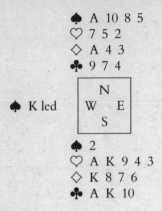

```
                    ♠ A 10 8 5
                    ♡ 7 5 2
                    ◇ A 4 3
                    ♣ 9 7 4
                           N
        ♠ K led        W       E
                           S
                    ♠ 2
                    ♡ A K 9 4 3
                    ◇ K 8 7 6
                    ♣ A K 10
```

'West leads the ♠ K against South's contract of 4 ♡. I am informed by reliable sources,' he went on, 'that there are in this country almost twice as many fishermen as bridge players. My partner on this hand from rubber bridge may well have belonged to the former category. He certainly didn't belong to the latter. See if you can do better than he did, but make haste. Those movements on the water's surface may well indicate that we are about to see some action.'

'It's started to rain,' I protested.

The club expert reached for a large multicoloured umbrella. 'So it has,' he said.

How should the hand be played?

Solution

It is a reasonable assumption that the trumps will break 3–2. As the diamonds are likely to divide 4–2 the declarer should aim to use one of dummy's small trumps to ruff his potential losing diamond. However, if he draws two rounds of trumps before conceding a diamond trick, dummy's trump may be extracted by the defender with three trumps.

26

Alternatively, if he draws only one round of trumps (or none) he may find that the defender with two trumps overruffs dummy. The solution is to duck a round of diamonds at trick 2. On regaining the lead, the declarer draws two rounds of trumps and then plays on diamonds, ruffing his last diamond, if necessary, with dummy's trump. The defence can only come to three tricks – a trump, a club and a diamond.

Complete deal

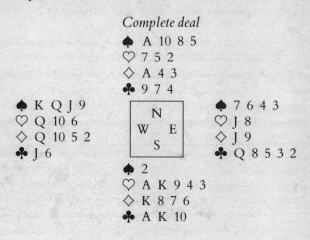

♠ A 10 8 5
♥ 7 5 2
♦ A 4 3
♣ 9 7 4

♠ K Q J 9
♥ Q 10 6
♦ Q 10 5 2
♣ J 6

N
W   E
S

♠ 7 6 4 3
♥ J 8
♦ J 9
♣ Q 8 5 3 2

♠ 2
♥ A K 9 4 3
♦ K 8 7 6
♣ A K 10

9

The ceiling consulter

'What goes on in their minds when they pretend they're thinking, I wouldn't like to guess. It's a complete mystery to me.'

The club expert was having his usual early evening moan in the bridge-club bar. 'I had one like that as a partner this afternoon,' he went on. 'Looked at the ceiling every five minutes as though he was expecting it to fall down. Towards the end of the rubber I was beginning to wish it would. "Look at your cards, not the ceiling," I told him. "The ceiling won't help you." If I said that once I must have said it a dozen times. To no effect, I might add, for look what he did to me on this hand.'

Angrily grabbing the nearest menu he scribbled down the following:

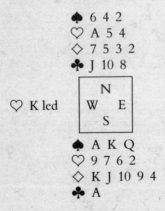

♠ 6 4 2
♡ A 5 4
◇ 7 5 3 2
♣ J 10 8

♡ K led

N
W   E
S

♠ A K Q
♡ 9 7 6 2
◇ K J 10 9 4
♣ A

West	North	East	South
			1◇
1♡	2◇	3♣	3◇
No bid	No bid	4♣	4◇
All pass			

'We were game and partscore and were pushed up to 4 ◇ by the non-vulnerable opponents. At least my partner was as South. Why he didn't double them in 4 ♣ I'll never know. Costs them 500 against accurate defence. Anyway, the opening lead was the ♡ K which he won on the table.

'"Not got much there, have you, partner?" he said, looking at dummy with the expression of a man who's been asked to clean up after the dog's been sick.

'At trick 2 he led the ◇ 2 and East produced the ◇ 8. Back went his head again and he gazed at the ceiling for a full two minutes before eventually playing the wrong card. One down.

'"Sorry, partner," he said. "Wrong view. It was a complete guess."

'Marvellous, isn't it? He knew the ceiling off by heart, but he didn't know which card to play from his own hand.'

Solution

The declarer must play the ◇ K from his own hand. The contract can't be made if East holds the ◇ Q. If the declarer plays the ◇ J, for example, at trick 2 and loses to the ◇ A, West would cash two hearts and lead another round, East overruffing dummy. The only chance, therefore, is to play West to hold ◇ Qx or singleton ◇ Q.

Complete deal

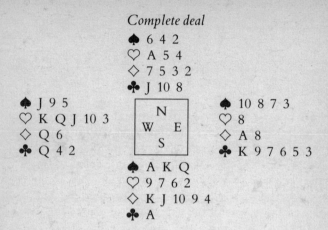

♠ 6 4 2
♡ A 5 4
◇ 7 5 3 2
♣ J 10 8

♠ J 9 5
♡ K Q J 10 3
◇ Q 6
♣ Q 4 2

```
    N
 W     E
    S
```

♠ 10 8 7 3
♡ 8
◇ A 8
♣ K 9 7 6 5 3

♠ A K Q
♡ 9 7 6 2
◇ K J 10 9 4
♣ A

10

The club expert goes down

The club expert was in an agreeable mood. Playing rubber bridge with three rabbits, he had attained vulnerability on the very first hand with a superbly executed double squeeze, listening with amused detachment as his opponents each rounded on the other for failing to guard the pivot suit. He was now about to clinch the rubber with a small slam.

'Thank you, partner,' he said as West led the ♡ J against his contract of 6 NT and dummy made its appearance. 'Just the shape I expected. You bid it well.'

♠ A 10 7 5 4 2
♡ Q 8 4
♢ —
♣ A Q 10 9

♡ J led

♠ K 3
♡ A K 5
♢ A K 9 7 4 3
♣ K J

The club expert took stock. Just another routine contract. Tricks to burn with a normal spade break. Pity there was little scope for his brilliant card play. Still it was going to be a sizeable rubber. Winning the opening lead in hand he laid down the ♠ K. West followed with the ♠ 6 while East impassively let go of a small heart.

A slight frown marred the declarer's features as he took mental note of the small red card standing out in sharp relief against the three black ones. After giving the problem a little thought he eventually led a low diamond at trick 3. This terminated his interest since West won with the singleton ♦ Q and persisted with hearts. Neither defender was under pressure and the declarer was restricted to the eleven top tricks.

Afterwards in the bar he was telling us about the hand. 'Would you believe it?' he said. 'Partner criticized my line of play. It was no use telling him I would have made the contract by force if either opponent had held ♦ QJ10 alone, or on a squeeze if West had held any four or more diamonds. He doesn't understand these things. I know that in the latter eventuality West could have broken up the squeeze by switching to the ♠ Q but they don't find defences like that in the game I was playing in.'

'How did your partner suggest you should play?' someone asked.

'It was laughable really. The fellow wanted me to cash all my tricks and hope for a mis-defence, like on the previous hand, as he put it. Still, that method is just about par for the course in a club like this. Usually works, too. No! The tragedy of the hand is that I would easily have made 6 NT if I'd played West for shortage in diamonds and not length.'

We looked at him. No one spoke. After all he was the club expert. But how would he have played the slam given a second bite at the cherry?

Solution

To make the contract the declarer needs to cash the ♦ AK at tricks 3 and 4 and continue with four club winners. This leaves the following position.

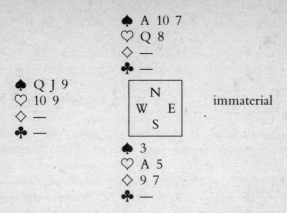

```
            ♠ A 10 7
            ♡ Q 8
            ◇ —
            ♣ —

♠ Q J 9        ┌─────────┐
♡ 10 9         │    N    │        immaterial
◇ —            │  W   E  │
♣ —            │    S    │
               └─────────┘

            ♠ 3
            ♡ A 5
            ◇ 9 7
            ♣ —
```

Declarer now plays two heart winners ending in hand and leads the ♠ 3. West is forced to split his honours and is left on play, conceding the last two tricks to dummy. In the diagram position West is unable to come down to two spades and three hearts as a spade winner can then be established with the ♡ Q as an entry.

Complete deal

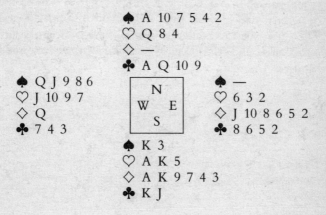

```
            ♠ A 10 7 5 4 2
            ♡ Q 8 4
            ◇ —
            ♣ A Q 10 9

♠ Q J 9 8 6    ┌─────────┐    ♠ —
♡ J 10 9 7     │    N    │    ♡ 6 3 2
◇ Q            │  W   E  │    ◇ J 10 8 6 5 2
♣ 7 4 3        │    S    │    ♣ 8 6 5 2
               └─────────┘
            ♠ K 3
            ♡ A K 5
            ◇ A K 9 7 4 3
            ♣ K J
```

11

An unconventional play

'An unconventional play,' announced a slightly inebriated club expert, 'may or may not succeed. Much depends upon the quality of the opposition. Nevertheless, an unconventional play in suitable disguise,' he continued, 'almost certainly will, since your adversaries will not be aware that they are involved in anything other than a standard situation. Put a bridge player in a standard situation,' he pontificated, 'and he will react in a standard manner.'

No one spoke. He took a large sip of brandy and continued.

'In this respect,' he said, still addressing his captive audience of one tired barman and myself, 'deception plays a major role. The hand I played earlier this evening in a contract of 3 NT admirably illustrates this precept.'

He paused for a moment and the barman took the opportunity to turn his back and began to polish glasses. The club expert took a gold-plated pencil from his waistcoat pocket and painstakingly wrote down the following hand.

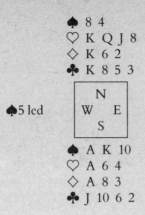

```
              ♠ 8 4
              ♡ K Q J 8
              ◇ K 6 2
              ♣ K 8 5 3
                 ┌─────────┐
                 │    N    │
    ♠5 led       │  W   E  │
                 │    S    │
                 └─────────┘
              ♠ A K 10
              ♡ A 6 4
              ◇ A 8 3
              ♣ J 10 6 2
```

'Now where was I?' he said, turning to address me. 'Ah! Yes! Against my 3 NT West led the ♠ 5 and East produced the ♠ J. Let me say at the outset,' he continued modestly, 'that I made a contract that would have defeated the majority of declarers. The reason I succeeded was because I made an unconventional play when at least one of the opponents was expecting the orthodox line.' Again he paused and I looked in the barman's direction. He was still stolidly polishing glasses. 'And if you are able to tell me what it was,' said the club expert with an intoxicated leer, 'I'll buy you a double brandy.'

'Not 'ere, you won't,' said the barman, suddenly springing to life. 'It's well past time. Can I have your glasses, gentlemen, *please*.'

That concluded the entertainment for the evening, but what was the club expert's line of play?

Solution

The declarer is attempting to establish a club winner before the defenders can take a possible three spade tricks. Nothing can be done if East holds both the missing club honours and the contract cannot fail if both these cards are with West. The problem is how to play the suit if the honours are divided since a mis–guess, with East winning the trick, is likely to result in defeat. The declarer should cross to dummy with a heart and lead a low club from the table. If this loses to West's ♣ Q, the safe hand is on play and spades cannot profitably be led. The play is likely to gain when East holds ♣ Qxx or ♣ Qx since it will be extremely difficult for him in second position to visualize what the declarer is doing. He is likely to play low and the ♣ 10 will force the ♣ A. This unorthodox line of play is the equivalent of playing West to hold the ♣ Q while at the same time giving East the opportunity to go wrong when holding ♣ Qxx or ♣ Qx.

Complete deal

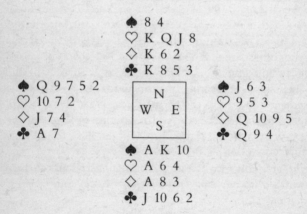

12

An ideal partner

'And so you see,' said the club expert, smiling benignly, 'that it is an important principle of my theory for the stronger player to use the weak notrump. The converse applies, of course, since his partner, as the weak link, is expected to employ the strong.'

It was early afternoon in the bridge club and the club expert was explaining his theory of variable opposites to the newest member.

'Moreover,' he continued, 'every effort must be made by the partnership to ensure that the better card player becomes the declarer, leaving the lame dog, as it were, to fulfil the equally important but less demanding role of guarding dummy.'

'That makes sense,' agreed his listener.

'These principles,' went on the club expert, 'are my scientific answer to those sceptics who . . . '

'*Table up*' came a loud cry from the far end of the room.

Reluctantly the club expert cut short his dissertation and, accompanied by the new member, moved towards the rubber-bridge game.

Later on that afternoon they faced each other as partners.

'Variable notrump?' asked the club expert.

'Yes, please,' answered the newest member. 'Naturally, I shall play the strong notrump and I should take it as a great honour if you would be kind enough to accept responsibility for handling the weak.'

'Most certainly,' smiled the club expert.

'Oh yes,' added the new member, 'as I am relatively inexperienced, may I leave it to you to take all the important decisions and, if possible, play all the hands?'

The club expert beamed. 'It will be my pleasure,' he said.

These niceties over, the first hand was dealt and the cards fell as follows:

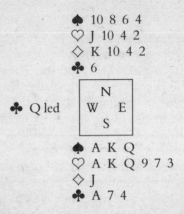

♠ 10 8 6 4
♡ J 10 4 2
◇ K 10 4 2
♣ 6

♣ Q led

N
W E
S

♠ A K Q
♡ A K Q 9 7 3
◇ J
♣ A 7 4

Afterwards the club expert was talking to us about his rubber with the new member. 'My partner played in 6 ♡ on this deal and received the lead of the ♣ Q,' he said. 'Such a charming fellow,' he went on, 'and so considerate. He did his utmost to steer the declaration into my hand but to no avail. The weight of the cards was against him. His heart suit was too strong and in the end he was forced to play there. The small slam is lay-down of course. I'm quite sure our new member is going to be a real asset to this club. He's the ideal partner.'

'He made the contract quite easily, then?' someone asked.

'No,' said the club expert, affably, 'he went one off.' He shrugged his shoulders. '*C'est la vie.* A slight mistake and it was all over. I'm not blaming him. The hand is a trap for players of limited ability.'

'What kind of an ideal partner goes down in a lay-down slam?' asked someone else.

'That he went down is not important,' he was told. 'It is what he picks up that interests me. Just look at his hand. And that was just the beginning. I've never seen such cards. We won the rubber with no trouble at all. The opponents were disgusted of course at what they called a prime example of beginner's luck. Naturally, I felt obliged to point out to them that there is more to it than that. Had they made an in-depth study of my theory of variable opposites they would have seen several such examples in the section headed "Good cards go to weak players". The converse is equally true since I myself usually hold rubbish. Still,' he added philosophically, 'don't we all?'

Meanwhile, how should the hand be played, and how did the declarer manage to go down?

Solution

At trick 2 the declarer should ruff a club in dummy with a high trump. Returning to hand with a heart he ruffs his last club with another high trump. He draws trumps and concedes a diamond to the opponents.

On the actual distribution he will go down if he draws one round of trumps before ruffing his losing clubs. After the second club ruff there is no way back to hand except with a high spade. This is ruffed by West who is void in spades and holds the three outstanding trumps.

Complete deal

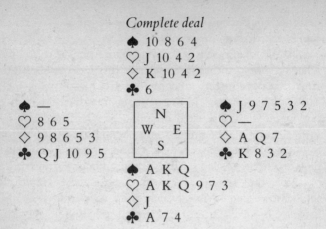

♠ 10 8 6 4
♡ J 10 4 2
♢ K 10 4 2
♣ 6

♠ —
♡ 8 6 5
♢ 9 8 6 5 3
♣ Q J 10 9 5

```
   ┌─────────┐
   │    N    │
   │ W     E │
   │    S    │
   └─────────┘
```

♠ J 9 7 5 3 2
♡ —
♢ A Q 7
♣ K 8 3 2

♠ A K Q
♡ A K Q 9 7 3
♢ J
♣ A 7 4

13

A tale of two deuces

'You mean to say you stopped in 3NT with 6 ♣ a spread?
You must be mad!' The club expert had turned out for us
on only a few occasions and had not yet mastered the art of
keeping his team-mates happy. 'Fortunately,' he went on,
'we got it back on the next. The declarer beat himself in
4 ♡. Plus 100.'

'Flat board,' I said miserably. 'I went down too.'

'I don't believe this,' said the club expert with some
exasperation. 'I thought you told me you took these league
matches seriously. What lead did you get?'

'The ♠ 2,' I said. 'My right-hand opponent won with
the ♠ K and switched to a low club to his partner's ♣ A.
As the cards lie they can always make a heart and a
diamond. I don't see what I was supposed to do.'

'You could try a bit of card reading for a start,' snapped
the club expert.

This was the hand in question.

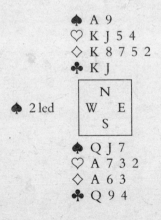

    ♠ A 9
    ♡ K J 5 4
    ◇ K 8 7 5 2
    ♣ K J

♠ 2 led   N W E S

    ♠ Q J 7
    ♡ A 7 3 2
    ◇ A 6 3
    ♣ Q 9 4

West	North	East	South
			1 NT
No bid	2♣	No bid	2♡
No bid	4♡	All pass	

Apparently the bidding and the play to the first three tricks had been the same in both rooms. The opening lead had been the ♠ 2. The declarer had played low from dummy and East had won with the ♠ K and switched to the ♣ 2. West took his ♣ A and continued the suit. How should the declarer play?

Solution

The defenders' play in the black suits would seem to indicate that both suits are divided 4–4. Each defender, therefore, has five red cards, a likely division of which is 3–2. The declarer should play off his two top hearts. If the ♡ Q does not appear he strips the hand by cashing his black-suit winners and the ◇ AK. At trick 11 he exits with a heart. The defender on lead (having only a doubleton diamond) is forced to concede a ruff and discard.

Complete deal

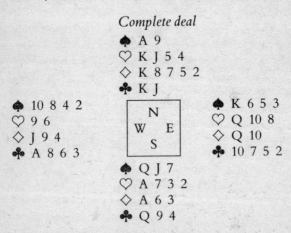

```
                    ♠ A 9
                    ♡ K J 5 4
                    ◇ K 8 7 5 2
                    ♣ K J
   ♠ 10 8 4 2                        ♠ K 6 5 3
   ♡ 9 6              N              ♡ Q 10 8
   ◇ J 9 4         W   E            ◇ Q 10
   ♣ A 8 6 3          S              ♣ 10 7 5 2
                    ♠ Q J 7
                    ♡ A 7 3 2
                    ◇ A 6 3
                    ♣ Q 9 4
```

14

Tuesday night blues

'It's incredible how they play sometimes,' said the club expert, wandering into the bridge-club bar late one evening and sitting down on a vacant stool. 'One minute they're on top of the world and the next they can't do a thing right.'

'I must say I agree with you entirely,' I ventured.

'From the way they perform sometimes you'd think they didn't want to win,' he continued.

'I frequently get the same impression myself,' I said.

'The needless penalty that was conceded just now was the last straw. I couldn't take any more. I simply got up and left.'

'You left them in the middle of a rubber?' I was genuinely horrified.

'I've no idea what you're talking about,' he snapped. 'Chelsea have just been knocked out of the Milk Cup and all you can think about is bridge. Still, if you're in that sort of mood I suppose I'd better humour you with a hand. Bridge is like a football match,' he philosophized. 'Both games abound with missed opportunities. Chelsea found this out for themselves tonight as did my partner on this hand from rubber bridge earlier today. He didn't exactly miss an open goal, but I dare say that, from the position in which he found himself, most good players would have hit the back of the net.'

Taking a blue-and-white programme from an inside pocket, he scribbled down the following hand.

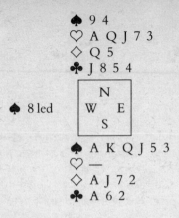

♠ 9 4
♡ A Q J 7 3
◇ Q 5
♣ J 8 5 4

♠ 8 led

N
W   E
S

♠ A K Q J 5 3
♡ —
◇ A J 7 2
♣ A 6 2

'Against South's contract of 4 ♠,' said the club expert, 'West found the best lead of a trump. East naturally played low and the declarer won in hand with an honour. How should he continue?'

Solution

At trick 2 the declarer should lead the ◇ J. If this is taken by the ◇ K, the ◇ Q is an entry for dummy's heart winner. If the opponents allow the ◇ J to hold the trick, the declarer should cash the ◇ A and hope to score game by ruffing a diamond in dummy. This line of play gives a better chance than leading a low diamond at trick 2 since, if the ◇ K is with East a trump return and tight defence will restrict the declarer to nine tricks.

Complete deal

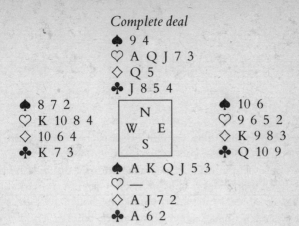

♠ 9 4
♡ A Q J 7 3
♢ Q 5
♣ J 8 5 4

♠ 8 7 2
♡ K 10 8 4
♢ 10 6 4
♣ K 7 3

N
W E
S

♠ 10 6
♡ 9 6 5 2
♢ K 9 8 3
♣ Q 10 9

♠ A K Q J 5 3
♡ —
♢ A J 7 2
♣ A 6 2

15

A touch of *déjà vu*

The club expert was vaguely uneasy. He had agreed to turn out for us in an away match and half-way through the evening found himself in a contract of 6 ♠, doubled by his left-hand opponent. This in itself was not remarkable. What troubled him was the hand he held, since he was convinced he had seen it somewhere before. There was something odd about the auction, too. That high pre-emptive bid on his right had a familiar ring. We all experience that 'I have been here before' feeling, but this time the vibes were extremely strong. It was, all in all, rather disturbing to say the least. Recollection tugged at his memory as the ♣ K was led and his partner tabled the dummy. This was the deal and the bidding.

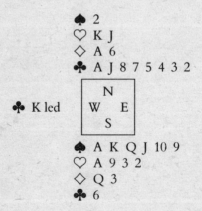

West	North	East	South
	1♣	5♢	5♠
No bid	6♣	No bid	6♠
Double	All pass		

The club expert stared at dummy in amazement. It was uncanny. The hand was a carbon copy of the famous deal played by 'Plum' Meredith over forty years ago in the same contract of 6 ♠ doubled. There had been an identical auction and the opening lead was the ♣ K. Meredith had won with dummy's ♣ A on which East had discarded the ♢ J. It was one of those rare hands where the exact distribution was available at trick 1. East had no black cards, nine diamonds and therefore four hearts. Plum had realized that the contract could only be made if West's heart holding was Q 10x. He had drawn all six outstanding trumps making the key discard from dummy of the ♢ A. He then finessed the ♡ J, cashed the ♡ K and exited with dummy's low diamond. East, with only red cards, was obliged to concede the last three tricks to the declarer. It was a beautiful hand, brilliantly played.

The club expert shrugged his shoulders. If it was his destiny to take star billing in this bizarre reconstruction, so be it. Solemnly he played the ♣ A from dummy at trick 1. To his utter astonishment East followed suit with the ♣ 9. When he had recovered from this setback, how did the club expert make the slam?

Solution

'Of course,' he said, as we were comparing scores at the end of the session, 'after the initial shock of seeing dummy, it was obvious that there had to be some logical explanation. Bridge history doesn't repeat itself to that extent. Clearly the boards had been used recently for some kind of par or set-hand contest and this particular board had escaped being redealt. Not through lack of diligence by anyone in our room,' he added, looking sternly in my direction. 'What really threw me was East following suit at trick 1. Now the contract can't be made by the Meredith line since West can be counted for four hearts. I therefore looked for a possible distribution that would enable me to make the slam and came to the conclusion that it could only be made if the original East/West heart holdings had been inter-changed. And this is indeed what happened during the post-mortem when they mis-boarded it. They wouldn't be too fussy about putting the cards back correctly if, for example, it was the last round. Here is the complete deal as it came to me.'

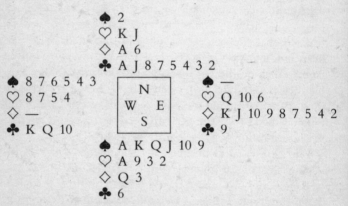

```
                  ♠ 2
                  ♡ K J
                  ◇ A 6
                  ♣ A J 8 7 5 4 3 2
  ♠ 8 7 6 5 4 3                        ♠ —
  ♡ 8 7 5 4        ┌──── N ────┐       ♡ Q 10 6
  ◇ —             W          E       ◇ K J 10 9 8 7 5 4 2
  ♣ K Q 10         └──── S ────┘       ♣ 9
                  ♠ A K Q J 10 9
                  ♡ A 9 3 2
                  ◇ Q 3
                  ♣ 6
```

'After drawing trumps, I led three rounds of hearts throwing the lead to East. He was end-played and forced to lead a diamond so I made the slam. Fortunately, it hadn't occurred to him to unblock when the heart suit was led.'

I looked at him admiringly. 'You know something?' I said. 'You're a marvel.'

'Quite,' he replied. 'And now we must press on. Unless the opponents are ready to concede, there are nine boards to play in the next set instead of the customary eight. I trust you are all familiar with the famous Belladonna hand? Just in case of accidents,' he added with a wry smile.

16

Curse of the Baron

'Why did I ever agree to play the wretched convention,' I said, perched on my favourite stool in the bridge–club bar during the interval between sessions.

'What's that?' some sucker asked.

'The remnants of a pint of beer,' I replied, 'but since it badly needs topping up, I'll gladly accept your kind offer of a refill. Meanwhile, let me entertain you with a bridge hand.' I rapidly jotted down the following:

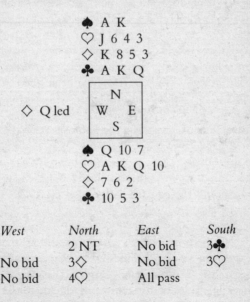

♠ A K
♡ J 6 4 3
♢ K 8 5 3
♣ A K Q

◇ Q led

♠ Q 10 7
♡ A K Q 10
♢ 7 6 2
♣ 10 5 3

West	North	East	South
	2 NT	No bid	3♣
No bid	3◇	No bid	3♡
No bid	4♡	All pass	

'As South you play in 4 ♡ after a Baron sequence,' I went on. 'All right, I know the hand is far too flat to use

Baron, but that's the way it went. West leads the ♢ Q followed by the ♢ J and you play low from dummy on each occasion. At this stage he refrains from continuing the suit, despite vigorous petering and nods of encouragement from his partner, so you rightly conclude that he is now without. At trick 3 he switches to a trump. What now?'

'That's OK,' said my drinking companion, after examining the hand for a full five minutes to make sure he had counted correctly. 'I take my ten top tricks. I should play for overtricks in a lay-down game?'

'Well worked out,' I said. 'Sorry, didn't I tell you? East is void in trumps. Makes it a bit tricky. Anyway, to cut a long story short, I did it your way, Frankie, hoping that West's six black cards were divided 3–3. They weren't. Unlucky hand, isn't it?'

'I don't think so,' said a quiet voice from behind me. I turned to see the club expert who had crept up unnoticed and was now eyeing the hand like an auditor scrutinizing a suspect balance-sheet. 'If you choose to bid in that ludicrous fashion when playing for money, that's your affair,' he went on, 'but you might at least have attempted to play the hand properly. There is another line, you know.'

'What is it?' I rashly enquired.

'A double whisky, please, if you insist. Your 100 honours will help to pay for it.'

'Good heavens! I forgot to claim them. What an idiot!'

'This time I agree with you entirely,' he said.

How should the contract have been played?

Solution

The declarer can make the contract providing that West's distribution in the black suits is no worse than 4–2. He should win the heart switch in hand and cash two top clubs and two top spades before returning to hand with a trump. At trick 9 he leads the ♠ Q. If West ruffs, the declarer overruffs in dummy and is able to cash the ♣ Q. If West follows suit to the ♠ Q the declarer should make the key discard of dummy's winning club and is able to take a high club ruff in dummy for his tenth trick.

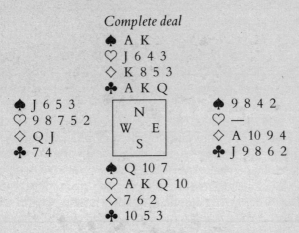

Complete deal

　　　　　　♠ A K
　　　　　　♡ J 6 4 3
　　　　　　◇ K 8 5 3
　　　　　　♣ A K Q

♠ J 6 5 3　　　　　　　　　　♠ 9 8 4 2
♡ 9 8 7 5 2　　　　　　　　♡ —
◇ Q J　　　　　　　　　　　◇ A 10 9 4
♣ 7 4　　　　　　　　　　　♣ J 9 8 6 2

　　　　　　♠ Q 10 7
　　　　　　♡ A K Q 10
　　　　　　◇ 7 6 2
　　　　　　♣ 10 5 3

17

ROM and RAM

The club expert was not well-versed in modern technology and had little idea of how computers worked. Consequently, he was mildly surprised when someone casually mentioned that nowadays they could be programmed to play bridge. At the time he formed a mental picture of robot-like figures sitting stiffly round the table, clutching playing-cards in steely tentacles and making bids in low metallic tones. Recently the image was rudely shattered when a computer expert started to play bridge at our club. He was an earnest, bearded young man who spoke learnedly of megabytes and used expressions like ROM and RAM. A systems analyst with a software company, he had been entrusted with the supervision of a new bridge program. It wasn't long before he started to tell us about the project. When the club expert discovered that all the computer could do was to follow its program, he was duly sceptical.

'I understand a computer being able to use standard bidding sequences,' he said, 'but in most auctions a certain amount of judgement is required. Put your machine in any bridge magazine's bidding competition, for example, and it would be hopeless. I doubt whether it would score even as many points as the editor. The same thing would happen in play,' he went on. 'It might be able to force out an ace or even handle a simple cross-ruff, but in more complex situations it would have no chance.'

Little more was said, but shortly afterwards the following hand was dealt and the systems analyst found himself playing in a contract of 6 $\heartsuit$.

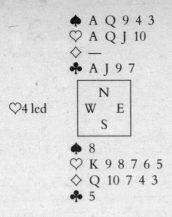

♠ A Q 9 4 3
♡ A Q J 10
♢ —
♣ A J 9 7

♡4 led

N
W   E
S

♠ 8
♡ K 9 8 7 6 5
♢ Q 10 7 4 3
♣ 5

A few days later the club expert told us about it. 'I was West,' he said, 'and naturally found the best lead of a trump against the computer Johnny's contract of 6 ♡. On this trick my partner discarded a low club. You can see from the hand that the declarer can make no more than eleven tricks on a cross-ruff. The contract can be made on another line, of course, but he mismanaged the play and went one down. The fellow then told us he was going home to feed the hand into his computer with the object of determining the best line of play. I could have saved him a journey but said nothing.

'The next day he returned triumphantly and told us that the computer had made the slam on a cross-ruff. "Impossible," I said, "it must have cheated." "Computers never cheat," he said sternly. I insisted that, on a trump lead, a cross-ruff would produce no more than eleven tricks.

'"Who said anything about a trump lead?" he replied. "With your hand the computer didn't lead a trump – it made the technically correct lead of the ♢ A."

'Marvellous, isn't it? What a pair! Talk about ROM and RAM. One of them can't play and the other can't defend. Naturally, I felt obliged to ask him to be sure to let me know when he was going to program the machine to play for money.'

How should 6 ♡ be played on a trump lead?

Solution

The declarer should aim to make twelve tricks with six trumps in his own hand, three diamond ruffs in dummy, two black aces and an established spade. Nevertheless, a certain amount of forward planning is required. It is essential for the declarer to win the opening lead in his own hand by overtaking with the ♡ K. At trick 2 he ruffs a diamond in dummy. He then plays the ♠ A followed by a small spade ruffed in hand. At trick 5 he ruffs a diamond in dummy and returns to hand with a spade ruff. Trick 7 is diamond ruffed with dummy's last trump and declarer again returns to hand with a spade ruff. He now draws the outstanding trumps and uses the ♣ A as an entry for the established spade assuming the ♠ K to have fallen after three ruffs.

Complete deal

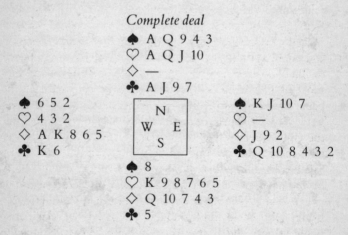

```
              ♠ A Q 9 4 3
              ♡ A Q J 10
              ◇ —
              ♣ A J 9 7
♠ 6 5 2              N              ♠ K J 10 7
♡ 4 3 2         W       E          ♡ —
◇ A K 8 6 5          S             ◇ J 9 2
♣ K 6                              ♣ Q 10 8 4 3 2
              ♠ 8
              ♡ K 9 8 7 6 5
              ◇ Q 10 7 4 3
              ♣ 5
```

18

The computer strikes back

During the weeks that followed we saw quite a lot of the systems analyst. We found him a pleasant, well-mannered young man who took a keen interest in his work and never found it too much trouble to explain in layman's terms some technicality involving computers. His bridge program was developing quite nicely and most of the members took a polite interest in its progress. The exception was the club expert who never lost the opportunity for ridicule when the subject of bridge-playing computers was raised. Not only was he completely devoid of interest but he went out of his way to make himself objectionable. He always referred to the analyst and his computer as ROM and RAM and constantly made jokes at their expense.

At the bridge table he pilloried the young man mercilessly and pounced on his every mistake. Because of his eminence the club expert enjoyed a certain amount of tolerance, but most of the members thought he went too far. One in particular, a chap called George Morgan who was an actor with the local rep, said quite openly that it was high time the club expert was taken down a peg. The trouble was that there was no one among our number who was capable of doing this. If it came to an argument about bridge he could have made mincemeat of the lot of us.

Late one afternoon the club expert came rushing into the bridge-club bar in high dudgeon. 'Look what that computer Johnny did to me on this hand,' he said, angrily scribbling down the following:

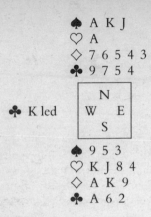

♠ A K J
♡ A
◇ 7 6 5 4 3
♣ 9 7 5 4

♣ K led

```
    N
  W   E
    S
```

♠ 9 5 3
♡ K J 8 4
◇ A K 9
♣ A 6 2

'He was in 3 NT and got the lead of the ♣ K. He held up the ♣ A until the third round – any fool can do that – and found that East had started with a doubleton club. ROM now managed to tie himself in knots and ended up one down. RAM would probably have done the same. Next hand the opponents bid and make a small slam and we lose a big rubber. The man's a complete idiot and shouldn't be allowed to play.'

'I can't agree with that,' George daringly remarked. 'I think he's very knowledgeable.'

'Knowledgeable? Are you serious? He doesn't know the first thing about bridge and that goes for his confounded machine, too.'

'That wasn't the impression I got the other night,' George went on. 'Did you see him on *Mastermind*? He chose 'The history of contract bridge from 1926 to the present day' as his specialist subject. Did extremely well, too. He was telling us afterwards that he had his computer to thank. He's programmed it with thousands of facts and figures about the subject and was able to use it extensively in preparation.'

'Those TV quiz programmes are all the same,' said the

club expert scathingly. 'They're a fix. If your face fits they ask you easy questions.'

'I wouldn't say the ones he got were particularly easy,' George said. He consulted a sheet of paper which he took from an inside pocket. 'How about this one? In the 1962 European Championships, Ladies' Section, who were the winners of the fourth round match between Iceland and Belgium?'

'I forget,' said the club expert.

'The computer didn't,' said George. 'What is the a priori probability of a 5–2 division of seven outstanding cards?'

'31 per cent,' replied the expert promptly.

'Wrong. 30.52 per cent. An answer to two decimal places is required. His computer is programmed to show seventeen, would you believe?'

'So what,' snapped the club expert. 'A fat lot of use that sort of information would be when it comes to playing the hand.'

'Now here's one you should get,' said George, grinning. 'An artificial bidding system currently in vogue in both Australia and Poland is known by name as the Forcing . . . ?'

'How the hell should I know,' said the club expert, trying hard to control his temper. 'Who cares what those foreigners do, anyway. Pass.'

'Correct. Still that's only one right out of three. Our systems analyst scored 100 per cent. We're really proud of him. Try this one. In the 1971 Vanderbilt Cup, an American . . . ?'

But the club expert, knowing when he was beaten, was already half-way towards the door. It was several days before we saw him again.

I happened to bump into the systems analyst about the same time. He was looking rather cheerful and told me that the club expert had just invited him to play partnership that evening. 'It's a great honour,' he said, 'but he's rather strange in some ways, isn't he? He keeps asking me to be sure to let him know when next I'm going to appear on TV. I told him I wasn't an actor, but he just smiled in a knowing way and said I shouldn't be so modest. What do you suppose he means?'

'I've no idea,' I said. 'Still, there's no point in worrying about it, is there? I expect he's confusing you with George.'

Incidentally, how should the declarer play the contract of 3 NT after holding up the ♣ A until the third round?

Solution

This is a simple exercise in communication. Clearly the diamond suit has to be brought in to make nine tricks, but if the declarer plays off his two top diamonds and continues with a third round he may find himself cut off from the ♡ K. Alternatively if he first plays off the ♡ A, cashes the ◇ AK and takes his ♡ K before exiting with a diamond, he may end up with five losers. The best line is to play the ◇ 9 from hand at trick 4. West can win and cash a club trick, but there is no further defence. The declarer plays the ♡ A before taking his ◇ AK. He then cashes the ♡ K and dummy is high.

Complete deal

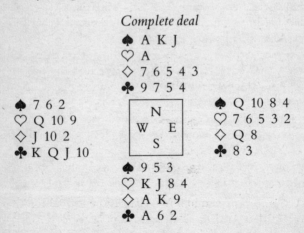

```
              ♠ A K J
              ♡ A
              ◇ 7 6 5 4 3
              ♣ 9 7 5 4
  ♠ 7 6 2          N          ♠ Q 10 8 4
  ♡ Q 10 9       W   E        ♡ 7 6 5 3 2
  ◇ J 10 2         S          ◇ Q 8
  ♣ K Q J 10                  ♣ 8 3
              ♠ 9 5 3
              ♡ K J 8 4
              ◇ A K 9
              ♣ A 6 2
```

19

The customer never talks back

'The game's getting too technical these days,' I announced, strolling into the bridge-club bar and plonking myself on a vacant stool.

The gaunt-looking individual on my left took a small sip of tomato juice but made no comment.

'Yes, they've certainly learned to hold up their aces when they can see dummy has no outside entry,' I went on. 'Takes them some time to work it out, mind you, but they get there in the end. Happened to me only this afternoon. Like to see the hand?'

This time a slight inclination of the head in my direction. Suitably encouraged I scribbled down the following:

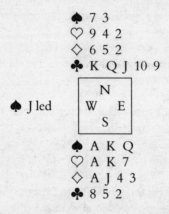

♠ 7 3
♥ 9 4 2
♦ 6 5 2
♣ K Q J 10 9

♠ J led

N
W E
S

♠ A K Q
♥ A K 7
♦ A J 4 3
♣ 8 5 2

'As South, I played in 3 NT against the lead of the ♠ J. Naturally I tackled the club suit, hoping to force out the ♣A in two rounds. These tactics smoked out the card's whereabouts in the form of two consecutive three-minute trances from my right-hand opponent. Regrettably, the ace itself did not appear and it now seemed that I would have to rely on diamonds for my ninth trick. As you can see, the suit itself is no great shakes. Short of padding, no intermediates, not enough stuffing – know what I mean?'

'I know exactly what you mean,' said my companion, speaking for the first time. 'No body.'

'That's it. That's it exactly,' I said, delighted by his perception. 'The only hope is a 3–3 break or a doubleton $\diamondsuit$ KQ. These contingencies didn't materialize so down I went – just like the *Titanic*. Next thing you know the opponents have won the rubber. It's enough to give you the needle.'

'It is indeed.' He got up from his stool and walked stiffly towards the door.

After he'd disappeared the club expert sidled over from a few places down the bar. He was grinning. 'I see you were having a few laughs with Jack the Lad just now. Kept you amused, did he?'

'And how! Not the greatest conversationalist, is he? Good listener though.'

'It's his job that does it,' the club expert said. 'He leads a quiet life. No one to talk to all day, you see. He's simply got out of the habit.'

'What is he? A Trappist monk?'

'No. Nothing like that. But in his line the customer never talks back. He's an embalmer. Has been for years. I thought you knew that.'

'Not likely. Would I offer him a hand? He might just take it.'

'He'd need more than that. All right, pass it along this way. I'll tell you where you went wrong.'

How should the contract have been played?

Solution

The declarer should play a low diamond at trick 2. On regaining the lead he cashes the ♢ A and turns his attention to clubs. If the ♣ A is held up for two rounds he switches back to diamonds. As the diamond lead is from the table, the declarer will come to a ninth trick whenever the suit is divided 3–3 or West's original holding was a doubleton honour.

Complete deal

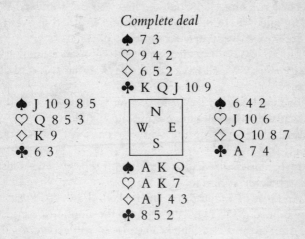

♠ 7 3
♡ 9 4 2
♢ 6 5 2
♣ K Q J 10 9

♠ J 10 9 8 5
♡ Q 8 5 3
♢ K 9
♣ 6 3

♠ 6 4 2
♡ J 10 6
♢ Q 10 8 7
♣ A 7 4

♠ A K Q
♡ A K 7
♢ A J 4 3
♣ 8 5 2

20

Those two-foot putts

The club expert walked scowling into the bridge-club bar and ordered himself a double whisky. 'I can't understand it,' he said, 'that's the worst afternoon I've had in I don't know how many years. Absolutely shocking.'

'Not to worry,' I replied, ever philosophical at another's misfortunes. 'We all have our off-days. What was it? Bad cards?'

'Bad cards? What on earth have cards got to do with it?' he snapped. 'Basically it's my putting, would you believe? I three-putted practically every green. Nothing would drop.'

'Is that all?' I asked. 'For a moment I thought you'd lost a few pounds at bridge.'

'And that's another thing,' he replied. 'I did. Afterwards they invited me to make up a four in the clubhouse for just one rubber, and I cut the worst player you've ever seen. Went down in every contract he played. Wouldn't allow me to play a hand, he said, in case my bridge was as bad as my golf. After he'd butchered one 3 NT contract that a babe in arms could have made I told the fellow that his performance was equivalent to missing a string of two-foot putts. "You should know," he said, and everyone roared with laughter. Most humiliating. Anyway, here's another hand he misplayed, though to be honest you might consider it more of a two-yarder.'

He quickly jotted down the following.

♠ 6
♡ K Q 5
♢ Q J 10 9
♣ Q J 9 6 4

♠ 5 led

N
W E
S

♠ A Q 10
♡ A 10 7 3
♢ K 5 2
♣ K 7 3

'My so-called partner played in 3 NT and got the lead of the ♠ 5, East playing the ♠ 7. Naturally, he went one down – what else? – though the contract's lay-down at trick 1.'

How should the hand be played?

Solution

The declarer must take precautions against East gaining the lead and returning a spade through the ♠ AQ before nine tricks are assured. At trick 2 he should cross to dummy with a heart and lead a low club from the table. If the declarer's ♣ K loses to the ♣ A, his spade holding is protected and there is time to force out the ♢ A. If the ♣ K holds the trick, the declarer should immediately switch to diamonds to make sure of his contract. The club lead from the table is best since, in the eventuality of East holding ♣ A108x, he is unable to rise with the ♣ A without giving the declarer sufficient tricks for his contract.

Complete deal

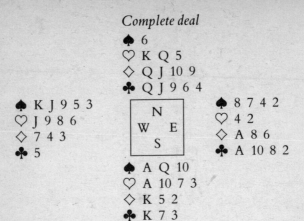

```
                 ♠ 6
                 ♡ K Q 5
                 ♢ Q J 10 9
                 ♣ Q J 9 6 4
♠ K J 9 5 3            ┌─────────┐            ♠ 8 7 4 2
♡ J 9 8 6             │    N    │             ♡ 4 2
♢ 7 4 3              │ W     E │              ♢ A 8 6
♣ 5                   │    S    │            ♣ A 10 8 2
                      └─────────┘
                 ♠ A Q 10
                 ♡ A 10 7 3
                 ♢ K 5 2
                 ♣ K 7 3
```

21

The bidding hog

By this time most of the regulars had become accustomed to the club expert's little foibles. They knew that he liked to play a dominant role in any partnership and were able to adjust accordingly. The game was as harmonious as could be expected, but sometimes the occasional visitor found his way to our doors. It was then that things started to happen. This was clearly demonstrated the other day when there arrived an impeccably-dressed smoothie with accent to match. He glanced around disparagingly until someone asked him if he was looking for a game of bridge. 'I should not be here were that not so,' he drawled. Nice use of the subjunctive, we thought. Obviously an English graduate. He went on to tell us that he was used to playing in first-class company and for high stakes, too. Our big game was somewhat low key by his standards, but it was the best we could offer and he agreed to play. As luck would have it, he cut the club expert in the next rubber and immediately skirted danger by treating him as a novice in the preliminary discussion about system.

'I think your best move is to tell me exactly what system you prefer to play,' he began. 'I can handle most of my customers. Have to in the game I usually toil in.' He spoke in low, soothing tones like an undertaker asking for a deposit.

The club expert, unused to being patronized, smiled grimly. 'Very well,' he said, 'if you insist. I play modified Chinese Precision with gamma responses, Cantonese Twos, King Fu over Threes. My deal, I believe.'

'Er . . . one moment, please. It's quite possible you may find me a trifle rusty on . . .'

'Then be kind enough to bid sensibly and avoid crass stupidities,' interrupted the club expert. 'Strong notrump. Cut please.'

Further attempts to elicit a system were met with either stony silence or inaudible replies and the newcomer eventually concluded that he was partnered by a harmless eccentric who had strayed inadvertently into the high-stake game. He decided that his best policy was to shield him from harm by hogging the bidding. This was his second mistake. A succession of wrong views and assorted standard errors did little to cement the uneasy alliance, particularly as each one was accompanied by a blistering volley of abuse from an irate club expert. The visitor was distinctly jittery by the time the following deal appeared.

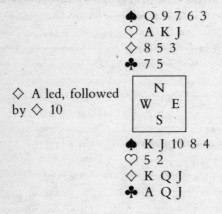

♠ Q 9 7 6 3
♡ A K J
♢ 8 5 3
♣ 7 5

♢ A led, followed
by ♢ 10

♠ K J 10 8 4
♡ 5 2
♢ K Q J
♣ A Q J

Afterwards the club expert was telling us about his misadventures. 'Look at this hand,' he said. 'As South my partner played in 4 ♠ and got the lead of the ♢ A followed by the ♢ 10. It was obvious that West had started with a doubleton and was angling for a ruff. One down. That sort of thing happened right through the rubber. I didn't get to play a single hand.'

'Well he could scarcely be blamed on this occasion,' someone said. 'He had to open 1 ♠. What else could he bid?'

'What's wrong with 1 ♣?' was the reply. 'Modified Chinese Precision like I suggested. I make the gamma response of 1 ♠ and he raises me to game. Simple enough.'

'The opponents can still manoeuvre to get a diamond ruff, though.'

'That may be,' said the club expert, 'but I still make the contract. So should he. 4 ♠ is lay-down played by either hand.'

How should South have played?

Solution

The declarer should eliminate hearts by leading the ♡ A, ♡ K and ruffing the ♡ J before touching trumps. East can win the trump lead and give his partner a diamond ruff, but West is then end-played, forced to concede a ruff and discard or lead into the club tenace.

Complete deal

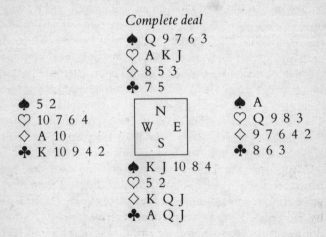

```
                ♠ Q 9 7 6 3
                ♡ A K J
                ◇ 8 5 3
                ♣ 7 5
  ♠ 5 2            ┌───────┐        ♠ A
  ♡ 10 7 6 4       │   N   │        ♡ Q 9 8 3
  ◇ A 10           │ W   E │        ◇ 9 7 6 4 2
  ♣ K 10 9 4 2     │   S   │        ♣ 8 6 3
                   └───────┘
                ♠ K J 10 8 4
                ♡ 5 2
                ◇ K Q J
                ♣ A Q J
```

22

Horse sense

'Making money at this game comes naturally to some people,' said the club expert, drawing on a large cigar and blowing the smoke leisurely into the air.

'So I'm told,' I replied somewhat coldly, 'but surely that's not the only consideration?'

'Of course not, my dear fellow,' he replied affably. 'I know your interest is not a pecuniary one. Heaven forbid! Nevertheless, financial considerations are a strong motivation for many people. Just look around and you'll see what I mean. Everyone here considers himself a potential winner, but that's just wishful thinking. Mark my words, by the end of the day most of the money will have found its way into a few select pockets. To be a winner requires more than good luck. It requires nerve, skill, patience, good judgement, flair and, of course, a profound knowledge of the game and its participants. And here they come now,' he cried, his voice rising in excitement as, amid the thundering of hooves and flying turf, the racehorses approached Tattenham Corner. The roar of the crowd increased in volume as the kaleidoscope of colour swept past, heading at breakneck speed in the direction of the winning-post.

'Well, that's the Derby over for another year,' said my companion when the hubbub had died down. 'I note that my selection was leading the field at this stage,' he added. 'As the colt is a strong finisher and a proven stayer, all that remains is for me to collect my winnings from Honest Joe. Your betting-slip will not be required, I fancy, so with your permission I will use it to jot down a hand I played

68

yesterday in a small slam. It should keep you occupied until I return.'

He quickly wrote down the following.

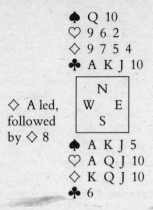

♠ Q 10
♡ 9 6 2
◇ 9 7 5 4
♣ A K J 10

◇ A led,
followed
by ◇ 8

N
W   E
S

♠ A K J 5
♡ A Q J 10
◇ K Q J 10
♣ 6

'As South,' he went on, 'I played in 6 ◇ and received the lead of ◇ A followed by the ◇ 8. East followed suit on each occasion. See if you can spot the best line. And that reminds me. Finesser's Nightmare is running in the next race. I think it would be most unwise of us to accept odds of less than 3–1 – don't you agree?'

He sauntered slowly away leaving me with a worthless betting-slip and a bridge hand. How should the slam be played?

Solution

The declarer can make the contract by locating the ♡ K either by a straight finesse or, after drawing the last trump and discarding two of dummy's hearts on spade winners, by a ruffing finesse. Nevertheless, a dummy reversal is the best line. Declarer should lead a club to the ♣ A at trick 3 and ruff a club in hand. He enters dummy with the ♠ 10 and ruffs a club with his last trump. He then re-enters dummy with the ♠ Q and draws the outstanding trump (trick 8). The remaining five tricks are a club winner, the ♡ A, two spades and the last trump.

Complete deal

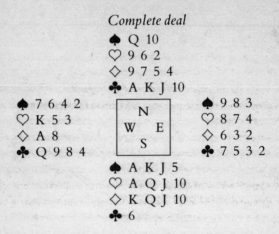

```
                 ♠ Q 10
                 ♡ 9 6 2
                 ◇ 9 7 5 4
                 ♣ A K J 10
  ♠ 7 6 4 2        N        ♠ 9 8 3
  ♡ K 5 3      W       E    ♡ 8 7 4
  ◇ A 8            S        ◇ 6 3 2
  ♣ Q 9 8 4                 ♣ 7 5 3 2
                 ♠ A K J 5
                 ♡ A Q J 10
                 ◇ K Q J 10
                 ♣ 6
```

23

The homecoming

'I suppose most players in this game have their pet aversions,' I philosophized, early one evening in the bridge-club bar.

The stranger on the adjacent stool turned to face me. 'What's yours?' he asked.

'That's extremely kind of you,' I replied. 'I'll join you in a pint. They serve an excellent bitter here. No, talking about aversions, the one type I really can't stand is the result merchant. I had one as a partner this afternoon, as a matter of fact. You play a little bridge, do you? Good. Have a look at this hand,' I said, rapidly jotting down the following:

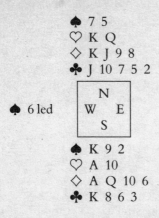

```
              ♠ 7 5
              ♡ K Q
              ◇ K J 9 8
              ♣ J 10 7 5 2
                  ┌─────┐
                  │  N  │
      ♠ 6 led     │ W E │
                  │  S  │
                  └─────┘
              ♠ K 9 2
              ♡ A 10
              ◇ A Q 10 6
              ♣ K 8 6 3
```

'As South, you end up in 3 NT and West leads the ♠ 6 from what looks like a five-card suit. East wins with the ♠ A and continues with the ♠ 10. You hold up until the third round, I suppose, and pitch a diamond from dummy?'

71

My new friend nodded.

'So what now?' I asked.

'Personally,' he replied, 'I would cross to dummy with a diamond and lead a low club, playing the ♣ K from hand if East follows low.'

'Precisely,' I said triumphantly. 'That's exactly what I did. You can't make the contract if West has a club entry so you play him to hold either ♣ Qx or singleton ♣ Q.'

'And what happened?' asked the stranger.

'What happened? I'll tell you what happened. My partner hit the roof because West showed void in clubs. That result merchant sitting opposite me worked out that I would have been able to pick up East's club holding for the loss of two tricks if I'd led the ♣ J. And didn't he let me know it!'

'Yes, most irritating,' agreed my companion, looking puzzled. 'But you still made the contract, I take it?'

I looked at him pityingly. 'Made the contract? My ninth trick has to come from the club suit and East is sitting over dummy with ♣ AQ9. How can I possibly make the contract?'

'I think something might be managed,' he said quietly. 'Look,' he went on, 'I've been overseas for a number of years. Only just got back, as a matter of fact. I've arranged to meet my brother here this evening for partnership. He'll be along any minute now. He's a bit too hot-headed to make a good player, but he's not a bad analyst. We'll see what he thinks. Ah! Here he comes.'

I turned to see the club expert in the doorway smiling broadly and setting off in our direction with outstretched hand.

'I suppose we'd better get him a drink to keep him happy,' whispered the stranger. 'Let's see, is it my round or yours?'

On winning with the ♣ K at trick 5 (West showing void) how should the declarer continue?

Solution

The declarer should cash his diamond winners leaving this position.

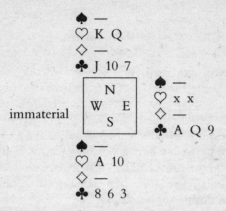

```
              ♠ —
              ♡ K Q
              ◇ —
              ♣ J 10 7
         ┌─────────┐      ♠ —
         │    N    │      ♡ x x
immaterial│  W   E  │      ◇ —
         │    S    │      ♣ A Q 9
         └─────────┘
              ♠ —
              ♡ A 10
              ◇ —
              ♣ 8 6 3
```

He now plays two rounds of hearts and exits with the
♣ J, forcing East to concede the last trick to dummy's
♣ 10. If, in the diagram position, East comes down to
three hearts and the ♣ AQ, the declarer plays on clubs to
develop a trick by force.

Complete deal

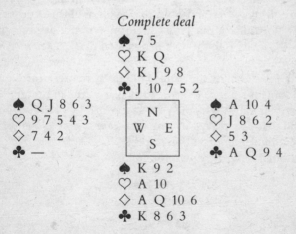

```
                    ♠ 7 5
                    ♡ K Q
                    ◇ K J 9 8
                    ♣ J 10 7 5 2
♠ Q J 8 6 3    ┌─────────┐      ♠ A 10 4
♡ 9 7 5 4 3    │    N    │      ♡ J 8 6 2
◇ 7 4 2        │  W   E  │      ◇ 5 3
♣ —            │    S    │      ♣ A Q 9 4
               └─────────┘
                    ♠ K 9 2
                    ♡ A 10
                    ◇ A Q 10 6
                    ♣ K 8 6 3
```

24

A question of form

'Well played, sir! Extremely well played,' cried the club expert, rising to his feet with enthusiasm as the overpitched ball went sizzling past cover-point's left hand and raced towards the offside boundary. It was the first day of the Oval Test and my companion, a life member of the Surrey CCC had invited me to join him in watching the England batsmen make hay in the late August of that sunless summer.

'Gooch and Gower are in tremendous form this afternoon,' I observed during the tea interval.

The club expert frowned slightly. For some reason my innocent remark had seemed to irritate him.

'True,' he said, 'but what is form other than the expression of a player's potential? I've never been too happy about the use of the word "form". A brilliant slip fielder, you will concede, may miss a relatively straightforward chance in one over and hold one twice as difficult in the next. Does this mean he is off form one minute and in form the next? I doubt it. It is potential that excites me. If a player is good enough, his potential is ever present, bubbling just below the surface and ready to break through at a moment's notice. This is particularly true in bridge. If you would kindly pass me your score-card I will show you a hand that was played in a match a few weeks ago and is not without interest in this respect.'

He quickly wrote down the following:

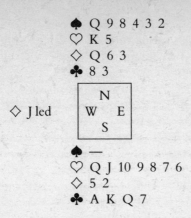

♠ Q 9 8 4 3 2
♡ K 5
◇ Q 6 3
♣ 8 3

◇ J led

♠ —
♡ Q J 10 9 8 7 6
◇ 5 2
♣ A K Q 7

'South opened 4 ♡ in both rooms and played there,' he
said. 'The ◇ J was led and held the trick, each declarer
playing low from dummy. Diamonds were continued and
East won trick 2 with the ◇ K. Instead of switching to
trumps he played a third round of diamonds. Incredibly
the defence was the same in both rooms. Each declarer
now had the opportunity to make the contract, providing
the clubs are not worse than 5–2. The first declarer gave
the opponents a chance to defeat the contract which they
duly accepted. The other declarer made no such mistake.
Perhaps I just happened to be on form,' he said with a
roguish gleam in his eye. 'See if you can spot the correct
line of play,' he added, 'but don't take too long. I see the
Australian fielders have taken up their positions and here
come the English batsmen. Judging from the applause,
you are not the only one who thinks they are in devastating
form.'

How was the hand played by (a) the club expert and (b)
the other declarer?

Solution

(a) The club expert ruffed the third round of diamonds
and played two top clubs. He continued with the ♣ 7

and ruffed with the ♡ K. The South hand was re-entered with a spade ruff and declarer's winning club was trumped with dummy's ♡ 5. The defenders could only make the ♡ A.

(b) The other declarer followed the same line of play up to ruffing the ♣ 7 with dummy's ♡ K. He then made the mistake of leading trumps. West was able to win and give his partner a club ruff.

Complete deal

♠ Q 9 8 4 3 2
♡ K 5
◇ Q 6 3
♣ 8 3

♠ A J 10 5   ♠ K 7 6
♡ A 2   ♡ 4 3
◇ J 10 9   ◇ A K 8 7 4
♣ J 9 6 4   ♣ 10 5 2

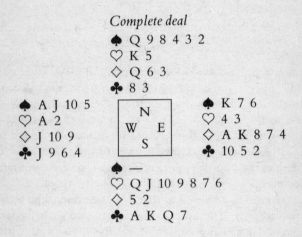

♠ —
♡ Q J 10 9 8 7 6
◇ 5 2
♣ A K Q 7

25

In pursuit of trivia

The club expert glanced at his watch with impatience. 'This is intolerable,' he said, 'it's nearly half-past eight and there still aren't enough players to make up a four.'

'What do you expect?' I replied. 'It's New Year's Eve. Most of the members will have made other arrangements.'

'Nevertheless, I think some consideration should be shown to those of us who do come here to play. I can see that I'll have to have a word with the committee. It's well over a week now since I had a game of bridge.'

'That's odd,' I said. 'Don't you usually spend Christmas with your niece and her family? I thought they were always pestering you to play with them.'

'True,' he replied, 'but this year some idiot gave them one of those boxed board games for a Christmas present. They spent most of the holiday playing with that. Trivial something or other, it was called, and that just about sums it up.'

'Pursuit,' I said. 'Trivial Pursuit. Very popular in some circles.'

'Not mine. If there's one thing I can't stand it's those games where you shake dice and move counters. Mind you, on the one occasion they did persuade me to play I wiped the floor with them. They asked me a ridiculously easy question at a critical stage and I won the game hands down.'

'What was it?' I asked.

'What is the meaning of the word triskaidekaphobia? I don't have to tell you that it's a morbid and unnatural dread of the number thirteen – a complaint not entirely unknown among certain partners of mine who seem to be completely incapable of counting a hand. However, speaking of trivia, there are many examples in bridge where a certain play, trivial though it may seem, is not without significance. One such instance occurred on Boxing Day, if I remember correctly.'

I looked at him sharply. 'I thought you hadn't played bridge at your niece's this year.'

'Once or twice we did. The Trivial Pursuit game went missing at one stage. No one could find it. Carelessness on someone's part, I suppose, but it left us with little alternative but to play bridge. Here, see what you make of this.'

He picked up a score-card and wrote down the following hand.

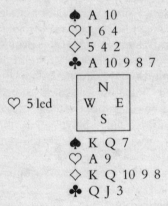

♠ A 10
♥ J 6 4
♦ 5 4 2
♣ A 10 9 8 7

♥ 5 led

N
W   E
S

♠ K Q 7
♥ A 9
♦ K Q 10 9 8
♣ Q J 3

'As South you end up in 3 NT, having opened the bidding with 1 ♦. West leads the ♥ 5. You play low from dummy, I imagine, and the first hurdle is successfully negotiated when East produces the ♥ Q. Winning with the ♥ A, you advance the ♣ Q. This loses to East's ♣ K and he returns the ♦ 7. Your ♦ K is headed by the ♦ A on your left. West, who happens to be my niece, gives the matter due consideration and returns the ♥ 10. What do you do?'

I studied the hand carefully. 'Is your niece capable of underleading the ♡ K in this situation?' I asked.

'Indubitably,' he replied. 'She has inherited a certain amount of avuncular talent.'

'In that case it's a complete guess whether I play her to hold the ♡ K or try to block the suit by playing low from dummy. I toss a coin. It's a 50–50 situation.'

'Then I regret to say,' said the club expert, 'that in the pursuit of trivia you are somewhere near the back of the field.'

How should the declarer play?

Solution

The declarer should treat East's diamond return at trick 3 as significant rather than trivial. It is, in fact, the key to the whole hand. Without the ♡ K, East, knowing that this card was well placed for the declarer would return a heart, hoping to clear the suit before his partner's potential diamond entry was removed. The fact that he returned a diamond is a strong indication that he himself holds the ♡ K. The declarer should therefore play low from dummy hoping to block the run of the suit in the event of a 5–3 break.

Complete deal

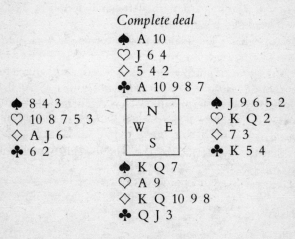

```
            ♠ A 10
            ♡ J 6 4
            ♢ 5 4 2
            ♣ A 10 9 8 7
♠ 8 4 3         ┌─────┐      ♠ J 9 6 5 2
♡ 10 8 7 5 3    │  N  │      ♡ K Q 2
♢ A J 6         │W   E│      ♢ 7 3
♣ 6 2           │  S  │      ♣ K 5 4
                └─────┘
            ♠ K Q 7
            ♡ A 9
            ♢ K Q 10 9 8
            ♣ Q J 3
```

26

Grand slam

The club expert sat hunched over his score-card, pencil at the ready. 'Why do I never hold cards like this at rubber bridge?' he said with some exasperation. 'Plus 2210,' he added, lighting a cigar.

Since his introduction to teams several months ago, he has developed a liking for this form of contest and nowadays is by no means averse to an occasional night out with the boys.

'You actually made the grand?' I was genuinely astonished. 'They stopped in six against us after a five-minute auction involving a series of relays, quantums and asking bids. How did you reach it?'

'With alacrity,' replied the club expert, who had little time for modern methods. 'Mind you,' he went on, 'it's an extremely good 7 ♡, but with the trumps breaking as they did I was fortunate that my left-hand opponent had a natural spade lead.'

'That's what I led against 6 ♡,' I said. 'It was funny really. When he saw dummy the declarer was furious with his partner for not putting him up to seven. He changed his tune though as soon as he touched trumps. Said that twelve tricks was the maximum on the hand whether it was played in hearts or notrumps. I'd love to see his face right now.'

'Perhaps I played it differently,' said the club expert with a sly smile.

This was the hand in question.

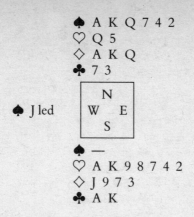

♠ A K Q 7 4 2
♡ Q 5
◇ A K Q
♣ 7 3

♠ J led

N
W E
S

♠ —
♡ A K 9 8 7 4 2
◇ J 9 7 3
♣ A K

How should the 7 ♡ be played after the opening lead of the ♠ J?

Solution

There are plenty of tricks unless the trumps divide badly, so the declarer should consider the possibility of making the contract in the event of a 4–0 trump break. Nothing can be done if West holds all four outstanding hearts, but it is possible to make the grand slam by means of a trump reduction play if they are all held by East. The declarer should start by ruffing the opening spade lead in hand and leading a low heart towards dummy's ♡ Q. When West shows out he returns a trump to hand forcing East to split his honours. Dummy is entered twice with top diamonds for two further spade ruffs, producing this position.

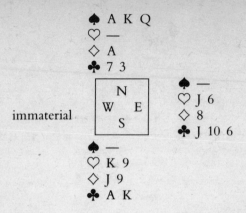

```
              ♠ A K Q
              ♡ —
              ◇ A
              ♣ 7 3
           ┌─────────┐        ♠ —
           │    N    │        ♡ J 6
immaterial │  W   E  │        ◇ 8
           │    S    │        ♣ J 10 6
           └─────────┘
              ♠ —
              ♡ K 9
              ◇ J 9
              ♣ A K
```

The lead is in the South hand and the declarer enters
dummy with the ◇ A and plays on spades, discarding
winners from his own hand until East ruffs.

Complete deal

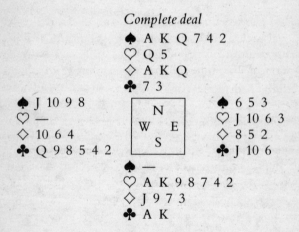

```
                    ♠ A K Q 7 4 2
                    ♡ Q 5
                    ◇ A K Q
                    ♣ 7 3
♠ J 10 9 8        ┌─────────┐      ♠ 6 5 3
♡ —               │    N    │      ♡ J 10 6 3
◇ 10 6 4          │  W   E  │      ◇ 8 5 2
♣ Q 9 8 5 4 2     │    S    │      ♣ J 10 6
                  └─────────┘
                    ♠ —
                    ♡ A K 9 8 7 4 2
                    ◇ J 9 7 3
                    ♣ A K
```

27

The trouble with finesses

'The trouble with finesses,' I said, 'is that when you really need one to work it's sure to be wrong.'

The man on the next stool nodded assent. 'You can say that again,' he said. 'Why, only this afternoon I was playing in 3 NT and . . .'

'A second point to remember,' I went on, 'is that whenever you make a safety play to land your contract, your partner is sure to point out that you could have made overtricks with the aid of a couple of finesses.'

'How very true,' he observed. 'Did I ever show you the hand where . . . ?'

'And the third consideration,' I continued firmly, 'is that even if a key card is well placed it sometimes can't be picked up because the opponent in question holds too many cards in that particular suit.'

My new acquaintance made no reply, having by this time run out of appropriate bridge stories.

'Take this hand I played in 4 ♡ this afternoon, for example. I needed the ♠ A to be onside or the heart finesse – and look what happened to me.'

I took out a scrap of paper from an inside pocket and wrote down the following hand.

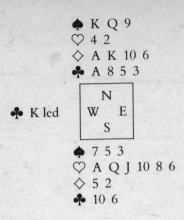

♠ K Q 9
♡ 4 2
◇ A K 10 6
♣ A 8 5 3

```
      N
  W       E
      S
```

♣ K led

♠ 7 5 3
♡ A Q J 10 8 6
◇ 5 2
♣ 10 6

'As South you play in 4 ♡ with this little lot,' I continued, 'and get the lead of the ♣ K which you take with
dummy's ♣ A. All right, I know that in certain circumstances it might be better to duck, but I can assure you that
with the distribution as it was it doesn't make a scrap of
difference. At trick 2 you take the heart finesse which
holds. You cross to dummy with a high diamond for a
repeat finesse and this time West shows out, discarding a
low spade. As you have a certain trump loser you have to
make two spade tricks, so at trick 5 you lead a low spade
towards dummy. East wins with the ♠ A and leads one
back so you end up with four losers. Unlucky, isn't it?'

My companion nodded. 'Yes, most unfortunate. Funnily
enough it reminds me of a hand I played recently in . . .'

'Absolutely diabolical,' came a loud cry from the doorway. I turned to see the club expert come striding into the
room, his face flushed with anger. 'The way they bid in
this place is a joke,' he announced. 'A grand slam they
made against me which only requires, would you believe,
two finesses and a 3–3 trump break. The luck of some
people is completely unbelievable. And what's more, they
didn't even have the grace to apologize.'

'Mine's the exact opposite,' I said, when he had calmed down a little. 'I was telling our friend here how I went down earlier today in this 4 ♡ contract.'

The club expert snatched at my scrap of paper like a mongoose launching itself at a cobra. He looked at the hand briefly, apparently without much interest, and then handed it back.

'Don't tell me, let me guess,' he said. 'Both the ♡ K and the ♠ A are offside.'

'No. The ♡ K is right, but I'll still bet you a drink you can't make the contract. It can't be picked up. It's guarded three times. East holds ♡ Kxxx. Surprised?'

'Only at your generosity,' he replied. 'The bet is accepted and I'll have a large scotch. I need it after that last rubber.'

How should the hand be played?

Solution

The declarer cannot be prevented from making the contract if he times the hand better. He should aim to take two heart finesses and manoeuvre to take two ruffs in his own hand. The play goes as follows. He wins the club lead, takes a heart finesse and returns to dummy with a high diamond to repeat the heart finesse. West shows out on this trick so the declarer returns to dummy with a diamond and ruffs a diamond in hand. Only now (trick 7) should he lead a spade which loses to East's ♠ A. The defence cannot prevent the declarer from entering dummy with the ♠ K for a further diamond ruff. He exits with a spade and makes the last two tricks with the ♡ AQ.

Complete deal

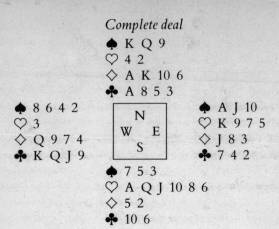

♠ K Q 9
♡ 4 2
◇ A K 10 6
♣ A 8 5 3

♠ 8 6 4 2
♡ 3
◇ Q 9 7 4
♣ K Q J 9

♠ A J 10
♡ K 9 7 5
◇ J 8 3
♣ 7 4 2

♠ 7 5 3
♡ A Q J 10 8 6
◇ 5 2
♣ 10 6

28

Mexican moonshine

'It's their use of completely meaningless jargon that irritates me,' said the club expert, taking a large swig of whisky and soda which so far had done little to improve his mood.

It was early evening in the bridge-club bar and a number of us had gathered there to watch one of England's televised matches in the 1986 World Cup. The commentators were beginning to warm up in the pre-match discussion. 'Arguably he's one of the finest players in their team,' one of them was saying. 'World-class, in fact, wouldn't you say?' 'Yes, indeed,' was his colleague's contribution.

'There you are,' said the club expert triumphantly. 'Can anyone here kindly tell me what "arguably" is supposed to mean in that context? Not one of that lot had even heard of the word a couple of years ago and now they use it all the time.'

'. . . and he's a yard faster than any striker the England defence have so far encountered,' continued the commentator, blissfully unaware of the criticism.

'Yes, indeed,' mimicked the club expert, 'if only one knew how fast "a yard faster" is meant to be. A shade slower than "a metre faster", I suppose.'

'England badly need a result here tonight,' said the commentator, suddenly changing tack, 'but if the players put 110 per cent effort into their game and increase their work-load by a further 15 per cent there is no reason why . . .'

'I can't stand much more of this,' fumed the club expert, 'the man's a raving lunatic.' He suddenly grabbed my arm and propelled me in the direction of a corner table. 'Let's get some sanity back into the proceedings,' he said. 'I want to show you a hand I played this afternoon in a contract of 3 ◇. You'll like this, I promise you. It's one of the most interesting part-score hands I've seen for a long time. We can go back to our seats as soon as the game starts.' Grabbing a table napkin, he wrote down the following.

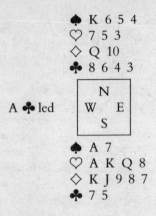

```
              ♠ K 6 5 4
              ♡ 7 5 3
              ◇ Q 10
              ♣ 8 6 4 3
                    N
  A ♣ led     W          E
                    S
              ♠ A 7
              ♡ A K Q 8
              ◇ K J 9 8 7
              ♣ 7 5
```

'I was South,' he said, 'and we were game and 40. For once I had a decent hand in this situation and opened 1 ◇ with confidence. West overcalled with 2 ♣ and this came round to me. Naturally, I tried 2 ♡, but West persisted with 3 ♣. My partner hesitated slightly and then bid 3 ◇. He was a little thin in values, but I don't blame him at the score and following my strong bidding. Anyway, 3 ◇ became the final contract. West started off with two top clubs and everyone followed, East petering. A third club was led which I ruffed. East discarded a low spade on this trick. How should I continue? You can see the problem,' he went on, 'the danger is that if . . .'

'And it's a GOA—L, came an excited cry from the television set. 'England have scored.' The club expert beat me by a short head in the rush to reclaim our seats as the commentary continued. 'It's uproar here. The manager is jumping up and down on the bench and the entire England team are completely over the moon. It's pandemonium.'

I glanced round to see how the club expert was taking this outburst. His face was flushed with excitement as he pointed towards the set. 'Just look at their goalkeeper. Have you ever seen such an expression?' he said. 'He looks as sick as a parrot.'

Incidentally, I never did find out that night what the danger was, but how should the hand be played?

Solution

On the bidding West is likely to hold the ◇ A. If the declarer attempts to draw trumps there is danger that it will be held up for one round. West will win the second round and force the declarer with another club. Control will be lost and the contract will fail if West started with ◇ Axxx. Alternatively, the declarer can try for a heart ruff in dummy. However, if a defender ruffs the third round of hearts, the lead of ace and another diamond will leave the declarer a trick short. The solution is not easy to see, but if the declarer cashes two winning spades, two winning hearts and then exits with a *low* heart, the defence are helpless. If the ◇ A and another are led, the declarer can win in his own hand and draw trumps. If the defence fail to do this the declarer can ruff his winning ♡ Q in dummy and lose only one diamond trick. Note that it is essential to cash two spades early in the play to prevent West from discarding a spade on the third round of hearts.

Complete deal

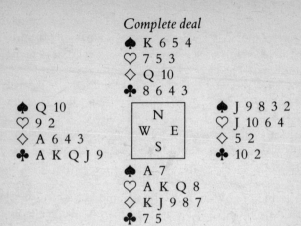

♠ K 6 5 4
♡ 7 5 3
◇ Q 10
♣ 8 6 4 3

♠ Q 10
♡ 9 2
◇ A 6 4 3
♣ A K Q J 9

N
W   E
S

♠ J 9 8 3 2
♡ J 10 6 4
◇ 5 2
♣ 10 2

♠ A 7
♡ A K Q 8
◇ K J 9 8 7
♣ 7 5

29

Just another flat board

'Sorry,' I said, as we rejoined our team-mates, the club expert and his partner, to compare scores. 'Humblest apologies. We let a game slip through on Board 11.'

No one spoke.

'Yes,' I went on, 'it wasn't easy for my partner to defend correctly. Very difficult, in fact. The declarer's line of play fooled him completely. They're not a bad team, you know. We may need to tighten up our game in the second half.'

'With you as a model that should be easy,' said the club expert. He looked at his partner and they both laughed.

'It's all very well to make jokes,' I protested. 'Wait till you see how the hand was played against us. I certainly don't blame my partner for being taken in.'

This was the hand in question.

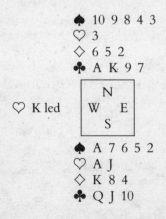

♠ 10 9 8 4 3
♡ 3
◇ 6 5 2
♣ A K 9 7

♡ K led

N
W   E
S

♠ A 7 6 5 2
♡ A J
◇ K 8 4
♣ Q J 10

West	North	East	South
			1♠
No bid	4♠	All pass	

I had been sitting West and led the ♡ K. The declarer won and played the ♠ A on which my singleton ♠ Q fell. He then tried the ♣ J to dummy's ♣ A, followed by the ♣ K dropping the ♣ 10 from his own hand. Dummy's ♣ 7 was now led. My partner who had been dealt a doubleton club and ♠ KJ looked long and hard at this and did a bit of squirming. He eventually discarded and the ♣ Q won.

Dummy was re-entered with a heart ruff and the winning ♣ 9 played. Whether or not East ruffed at this stage was immaterial. South was able to discard a losing diamond and lost only three tricks.

The club expert looked up from his score-card. 'I take it you petered in clubs,' he said.

'I'm afraid not. I had four tiny ones. I didn't think it mattered.'

'This is completely unbelievable,' he said, angrily stubbing out his cigar on a near-by pot plant. How do you expect your partner to defend correctly if you insist on giving him the wrong count? All you have to do is peter and the declarer can be counted for three clubs. His club play becomes immediately suspect and your partner has no difficulty in ruffing the third round and switching to diamonds. The defence then take three diamonds and a spade. Congratulations! You turned a 10-point swing into another flat board.'

'Thank goodness you made it,' I said. 'You took the same line, I suppose?'

The club expert fixed me with a steely glare. 'I trust you're not serious?' he said.

How should the hand be played?

Solution

The club expert gave himself an extra chance by having the first trump lead come from the table. At trick 2 he led the ♣ J and won with dummy's ♣ A. He now led the ♠ 3, playing low from hand when East produced the ♠ J. West was obliged to win with the ♠ Q and had no good return. The declarer was able to draw the outstanding trump and discard a losing diamond on the fourth club. Although the line of play is not foolproof, it gives the declarer the best chance. On the actual distribution East would have to defend extremely smartly to rise with the ♠ K when the trump lead came from the table.

Complete deal

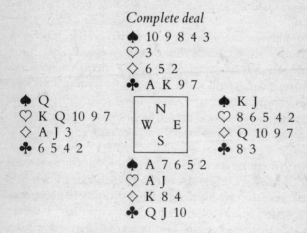

```
            ♠ 10 9 8 4 3
            ♡ 3
            ◇ 6 5 2
            ♣ A K 9 7
♠ Q                      N              ♠ K J
♡ K Q 10 9 7      W          E         ♡ 8 6 5 4 2
◇ A J 3                  S              ◇ Q 10 9 7
♣ 6 5 4 2                               ♣ 8 3
            ♠ A 7 6 5 2
            ♡ A J
            ◇ K 8 4
            ♣ Q J 10
```

30

I remember it well

'Like the poor and the sick,' said the club expert, 'opponents' mistakes will always be with us.' He took a thoughtful sip of his dry martini and lemonade and lit a fresh cigar.

I looked up from my beer. 'That sentiment's been expressed before. I can remember reading it somewhere,' I said.

'Possibly,' agreed the club expert affably. 'Bridge scribes are constantly pursuing this theme. Nevertheless, insufficient research has yet been made. Perhaps one of these days the balance will shift. It was S. J. Simon, I believe, who first drew our attention to opponents' mistakes and suggested that the good player should go out of his way to encourage them. That was BYT, I expect.'

'BYT?'

'An Americanism I picked up. Short for "before your time". However, although it is generally agreed that you should give the opponents every opportunity to go wrong, most writers seem to hold the strange view that all defenders are of equal strength. Nothing could be further from the truth. My "Theory of Variable Opposites" proves conclusively that one player in every partnership is usually stronger than the other. It makes sense, therefore, to direct your attention towards the weaker link. This should even influence you when it comes to choice of seats. I have heard it said that if you are playing against two opponents of unequal ability it is good tactics to sit over the weaker player – so that you can double him if he steps out of line, I suppose.

'My own views are the complete opposite. Given the choice, I prefer to sit on the tyro's right in which position I can confuse him with my bidding. More often than not I end up as the declarer, and then the opening lead comes up to me from the poorer player. I have never found this to be a disadvantage. Anyone can double an overbidder, but it takes an artiste to land an impossible contract by giving a mediocre opponent the opportunity to make a standard play. Perhaps you remember this hand I played against you in a contract of 4 ♡ shortly after you became a member here. You were sitting on my left, I believe, and opened 1 ♠.'

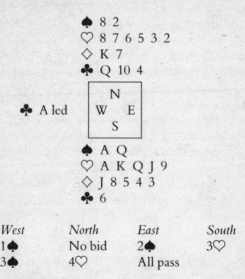

```
              ♠ 8 2
              ♡ 8 7 6 5 3 2
              ◇ K 7
              ♣ Q 10 4
                   N
  ♣ A led       W     E
                   S
              ♠ A Q
              ♡ A K Q J 9
              ◇ J 8 5 4 3
              ♣ 6
```

West	North	East	South
1♠	No bid	2♠	3♡
3♠	4♡	All pass	

'Against my contract of 4 ♡,' continued the club expert, 'you led the ♣ A to which your partner contributed the ♣ 2. You gave the matter due consideration and switched to the ♡ 10 and your partner followed suit with the ♡ 4. So far you have defended impeccably, but were unprepared for what was to come and allowed me to make the contract. You recall your mistake, I expect?'

'To quote GBS,' I replied, 'NBL.'

How was the contract played?

Solution

The obvious line of play is to lead diamonds, trusting that the ♢ A is well-placed. In this eventuality the declarer will probably make eleven tricks since, if they divide no worse than 4–2, he will be able to establish a long diamond for a spade discard in dummy. However, the contract will fail if the ♢ A is offside since a spade return from East will ensure four tricks for the defence. The declarer therefore does best to tackle the diamond suit by leading the ♢ J from hand at trick 3. If West plays low he takes the normal line of playing dummy's ♢ K. West, however, may cover with the ♢ Q. In these circumstances the contract is lay-down. The ♢ Q is allowed to hold and, with the safe hand on lead, there is time to set up a long diamond for a spade discard from dummy. In the eventuality of the ♢ Q being singleton, West is end-played. Note that it is extremely difficult for West to refuse to cover the ♢ J when, for example, he has been dealt ♢ Q10 or ♢ Q10x.

Complete deal

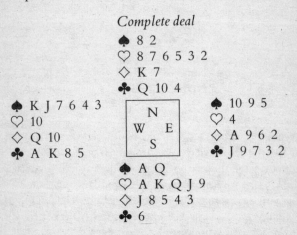

♠ 8 2
♡ 8 7 6 5 3 2
♢ K 7
♣ Q 10 4

♠ K J 7 6 4 3
♡ 10
♢ Q 10
♣ A K 8 5

♠ 10 9 5
♡ 4
♢ A 9 6 2
♣ J 9 7 3 2

♠ A Q
♡ A K Q J 9
♢ J 8 5 4 3
♣ 6

31

Snookered

The club expert looked at me from across the table. 'I can't say I'm over-impressed if that's your idea of safety play,' he said.

'It was a difficult shot,' I protested. 'The cue-ball was right up against the cushion.'

'Nevertheless, you could have done far better. Take more time before you play,' he advised. 'Surely I don't have to tell you of all people. Hasty play, and all that . . . . '

'This table's hopeless,' I said petulantly. 'The cloth won't take deep screw and there's a definite slope towards the pockets at the baulk end.'

'The former will scarcely affect your game as I remember it,' said the club expert, 'and the latter can only improve it.' He squinted at the green cloth from several angles before challking his cue and preparing for his shot. 'You've only yourself to blame,' he said, as the red ball rolled slowly across the table, hung tantalizingly over the centre pocket, and gently dropped. 'Why didn't you snooker me two shots ago when you had the chance? Instead you decided to take on that long red – a shot which had about as much chance of success as a ballet dancer with a wooden leg. You never learn from your mistakes, do you? It was a carbon copy of this afternoon's performance, if I remember correctly.'

'You don't,' I said triumphantly. 'We didn't play snooker this afternoon. We played bridge.'

'Quite. I was recalling the 3 NT contract you should have made. Remember the hand? I was sitting on your right and you had the perfect opportunity to put me in an impossible position – to snooker me in other words. However, you let me off the hook and eventually went one down.'

This is the hand to which he was referring.

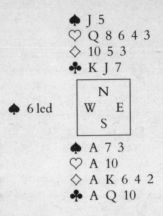

♠ J 5
♡ Q 8 6 4 3
♢ 10 5 3
♣ K J 7

♠ 6 led

N
W   E
S

♠ A 7 3
♡ A 10
♢ A K 6 4 2
♣ A Q 10

As South I had played in 3 NT and received the lead of the ♠ 6. I tried dummy's ♠ J without much hope of success and the club expert covered with the ♠ Q. Naturally, I played low from the South hand and the ♠ 9 was continued. I ducked again but was forced to win the third round when the club expert persisted with the ♠ 2. The play in the spade suit seemed to indicate that West had started with five. How should the declarer continue?

Solution

Declarer's problem is to establish the diamond suit without allowing West to gain the lead since he is marked with two winning spades. Nothing can be done if West holds ♢ Qxx, but the declarer can guard against ♢ Jxx by leading the suit twice from dummy. At trick 4 he crosses to dummy with a club and leads a low diamond. If East plays low the declarer wins in hand and again returns to dummy with a club to lead a further diamond. When East's ♢ Q appears it is allowed to hold the trick. Note that it is not good enough to play a high diamond from hand at trick 4. An astute East will unblock with the ♢ Q, thereby creating an entry for his partner. Playing the suit from dummy prevents this since, as soon as the ♢ Q appears, it is allowed to hold the trick.

Complete deal

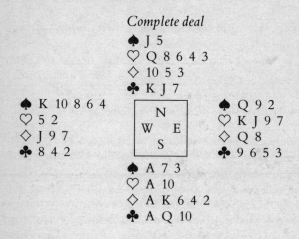

```
              ♠ J 5
              ♡ Q 8 6 4 3
              ♢ 10 5 3
              ♣ K J 7
♠ K 10 8 6 4      N       ♠ Q 9 2
♡ 5 2        W       E    ♡ K J 9 7
♢ J 9 7           S       ♢ Q 8
♣ 8 4 2                   ♣ 9 6 5 3
              ♠ A 7 3
              ♡ A 10
              ♢ A K 6 4 2
              ♣ A Q 10
```

32

In praise of conventions

'Don't ask me,' said the club expert, 'why bridge players go to out-of-season seaside resorts to compete against others who come into the bidding on tram tickets and have a convention for every day of the year. Just don't ask me.'

'All right,' I said, 'I won't ask you.' He knew I had just arrived back from Eastbourne and was trying to wind me up.

'So much scientific twaddle is being introduced into the game these days that it's getting ridiculous,' he went on. 'I wouldn't care if the gadgets were any good, but they usually give away so much information that the declarer can't help making his contract. When the players eventually realize this, the convention is discarded to be replaced by another equally ridiculous. The original convention disappears completely. No one knows what happens to it. It just vanishes.'

'It "vanishes like snow upon the desert's dusty face" as Omar once said,' I murmured.

'Omar Sharif? Now there's a player. And he was right, too.'

'Different Omar. Mine never played. He had problems enough without.'

'Then he should have learned. It would have taken his mind off them,' said the club expert who was no literary giant. 'But enough of this tittle-tattle,' he went on, 'What are you waiting for?'

'Pardon?'

'Hands. You must have some bridge hands to show me. I take it you did get round to playing cards this week-end?'

'Certainly,' I replied. 'See what you make of this.'

Taking an old score-card from my jacket pocket I wrote down the following.

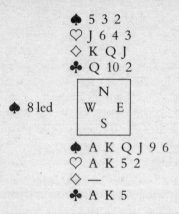

♠ 5 3 2
♡ J 6 4 3
♢ K Q J
♣ Q 10 2

♠ 8 led

N
W E
S

♠ A K Q J 9 6
♡ A K 5 2
♢ —
♣ A K 5

'So you reach 6 ♠ with this lot and the opening lead is the ♠ 8. How do you play the slam?' I said quickly.

The club expert studied the hand intently. No lightning analysis this time, I noticed.

'Any adverse bidding?' he eventually enquired.

'Funny you should ask that,' I said. 'Naturally, I opened 2 ♣ with the South hand. As it happened, West entered the fray with a bid of 2 ♠.'

'Aha! So you think you can catch me out,' said the club expert. 'What did I tell you? They come in on tram tickets. It's the sea air that does it. That and the favourable vulnerability, I suppose. And the meaning?'

'Upon enquiry, it was explained at the table that the 2 ♠ bid shows a distributional hand with a singleton spade and at least five cards in each of two unspecified suits. The total high-card point count was said to be between 5 and 7.'

'In which case,' said the club expert, 'I spread my hand after the opening lead and claim twelve tricks – thirteen if West holds the doubleton ♡ Q. I feel that one should not waste time in a pairs event. It's unfair to the other players. The contract is lay-down, of course, providing West has the values that were advertised. And if he hasn't,' he added darkly, 'I call the sheriff. Next hand please.'

How should the slam be played?

Solution

On the bidding, West is marked with the ♢ A and either the ♡ Q or the ♣ J. The declarer should draw trumps and play off the ♡ AK. If West has long hearts (or the singleton ♡ Q), dummy's ♡ J is the twelfth trick. If West shows up with shortage in hearts the declarer should play a top club from hand followed by a low club, finessing the ♣ 10 if West plays low. He then plays dummy's ♢ K, discarding the remaining high club from hand. West cannot escape the end-play and is obliged to concede an entry to dummy.

Complete deal

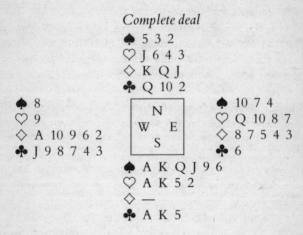

```
              ♠ 5 3 2
              ♡ J 6 4 3
              ♢ K Q J
              ♣ Q 10 2
♠ 8                          ♠ 10 7 4
♡ 9              N           ♡ Q 10 8 7
♢ A 10 9 6 2  W   E          ♢ 8 7 5 4 3
♣ J 9 8 7 4 3     S          ♣ 6
              ♠ A K Q J 9 6
              ♡ A K 5 2
              ♢ —
              ♣ A K 5
```

33

A bag of crisps to go with it

'Why is it,' I said, 'that in this game, whenever you hit a losing streak it seems to last twice as long as a winning one?'

I was sitting by chance in the bridge-club bar at the conclusion of the afternoon's entertainment. The morose-looking individual on the next stool looked up from his beer.

'You never spoke a truer word,' he said. 'In the last few weeks I've lost a fortune in this place. My luck at the moment is diabolical. Is yours the same?'

'That's extremely generous of you,' I said. 'Certainly, if you're sure the old purse-strings can stretch to it. I'll join you in a pint. And another thing,' I went on, warming to my theme, 'have you noticed that if you're playing out of luck things start to happen. Have you noticed that? The opponents always seem to defend better for a start. Take this afternoon for instance, I was playing in 4 ♠ with this lot.'

I scribbled down the following hand on a beer-mat.

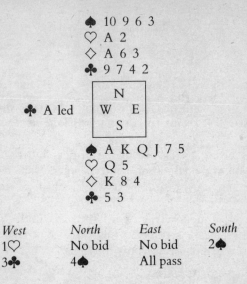

♠ 10 9 6 3
♡ A 2
♢ A 6 3
♣ 9 7 4 2

♣ A led

N
W E
S

♠ A K Q J 7 5
♡ Q 5
♢ K 8 4
♣ 5 3

West	North	East	South
1♡	No bid	No bid	2♠
3♣	4♠	All pass	

'You can see from the auction that West has done his share of bidding and is marked with a good hand. He started off with three top clubs and I ruffed the third round. East threw a low heart on this trick so there is a fairly good count right away. The hand is a baby end-play, isn't it? I drew trumps ending in dummy – incidentally West didn't have any – and ruffed the last club. I then played ♢ A, ♢ K and a third round hoping that West would win and would have to give me a ruff and discard or lead a heart. Well West didn't win. He unblocked from ♢ Qxx without batting an eyelid and I had to go one down. You play the same way, don't you?'

'More or less,' agreed my gloomy companion. 'Mind you,' he went on, 'you could have been a shade more subtle. I read somewhere that in a situation like this if you cash the ♢ AK early on you might catch your opponent off guard.'

'I doubt whether that would have made much difference,' I said. 'He could have ditched the $\diamondsuit$ Q when I drew trumps. I saw this particular defender studying a book on end-plays the other week. Half the trouble is that some people read far too much about the game these days.'

'And others don't read enough.'

I turned to see the club expert who had quietly crept up behind me and was now scrutinizing the hand like a terrier eyeing a rat-hole.

'Look,' he said, 'once you decide to play West for the $\heartsuit$ K there's really only one line worth considering, isn't there?'

'What is it?' I asked, unguardedly.

'The usual, please. Oh, and a bag of crisps to go with it. Bridge lessons come expensive.'

How should the hand be played?

Solution

After ruffing the third round of clubs declarer should play off all his trumps to produce this position.

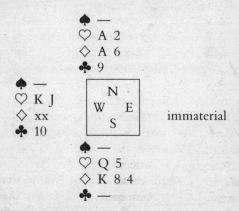

He now plays two rounds of diamonds ending in dummy and throws West in with a club to lead away from the ♡K. In the diagram position West is unable to keep three diamonds without either unguarding the ♡ K or discarding his winning club.

Complete deal

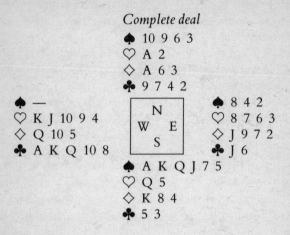

```
              ♠ 10 9 6 3
              ♡ A 2
              ♢ A 6 3
              ♣ 9 7 4 2
♠ —                         ♠ 8 4 2
♡ K J 10 9 4      N         ♡ 8 7 6 3
♢ Q 10 5       W     E      ♢ J 9 7 2
♣ A K Q 10 8      S         ♣ J 6
              ♠ A K Q J 7 5
              ♡ Q 5
              ♢ K 8 4
              ♣ 5 3
```

34

Finishing power

On many occasions in the past I had been impressed by the club expert's remarkable powers of concentration. Not that there was ever any outward evidence of this. To the casual observer his calm exterior betrayed nothing. However, from past experience I was aware of the mental effort he put into his game. The present situation, I knew, would tax his qualities to the full. I watched intently as he glanced first at the board, then at the score and finally back to the board. His mind made up, he sprang rapidly into action. The dart left his hand with the swiftness of an arrow and thudded into the dartboard, clipping the wire just inside the 16. 'Double 8 left,' he said. Again he threw and this time the missile, with a resounding thump, embedded itself in the target.

'Good shot,' I said, genuinely surprised.

'Thank you. My game, I believe. You will doubtless be aware from watching TV,' he continued, 'how many of the professional darts players incline to leave a double 16 finish. The reason for this is, of course, that if the first dart hits the single, as did mine, then only a slight adjustment is required for an almost identical shot. An extra chance, as it were, in bridge parlance. Nevertheless, concentration is the hallmark of the top-class player. A fellow I cut in the rubber-bridge game this afternoon would have done well to remember this. Here is a hand that he butchered.'

Cleaning the board with a damp cloth he picked up a piece of chalk and wrote down the following.

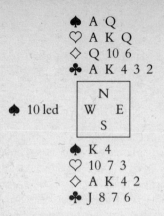

```
            ♠ A Q
            ♡ A K Q
            ◇ Q 10 6
            ♣ A K 4 3 2
                  ┌─────────┐
                  │    N    │
  ♠ 10 led        │  W   E  │
                  │    S    │
                  └─────────┘
            ♠ K 4
            ♡ 10 7 3
            ◇ A K 4 2
            ♣ J 8 7 6
```

'As North I opened 2 ♣,' he went on, 'and my partner responded in notrumps, thereby reducing me to the role of helpless spectator. I could do no less, you will agree, than raise him to 6 NT which is where he played, receiving the lead of the ♠ 10. Whether he was a darts player was not revealed at this stage, but his lack of concentration was, since he went down in what is essentially an easy contract. See if you can do better, but make haste,' he added, as a burly individual in shirt-sleeves brushed past us and gazed at the score-board in evident disbelief. 'It seems that some-one is about to challenge the winner.'

How should the slam be played?

Solution

The lead of a low club at trick 2 will guarantee four club tricks against any distribution. If East shows void the declarer plays ♣ J losing to West's ♣ Q. Declarer wins the spade continuation and crosses to the ◇ A. The lead of the ♣ 8 forces a cover from West. Dummy wins and returns a diamond. Declarer leads the ♣ 7, again forcing West to cover. The ♣ 6 draws the ♣ 5 and the dummy hand is high.

Complete deal

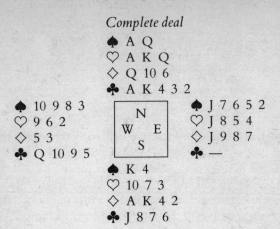

```
              ♠ A Q
              ♡ A K Q
              ◇ Q 10 6
              ♣ A K 4 3 2
♠ 10 9 8 3        N        ♠ J 7 6 5 2
♡ 9 6 2      W       E     ♡ J 8 5 4
◇ 5 3             S        ◇ J 9 8 7
♣ Q 10 9 5                 ♣ —
              ♠ K 4
              ♡ 10 7 3
              ◇ A K 4 2
              ♣ J 8 7 6
```

35

The captain's table

'How many times do I have to tell you? Don't bid these slams unless you're going to make them. That way we don't lose points.'

The club expert had been playing in our league matches for several months now, and had recently appointed himself team captain. Not that he ever concerned himself with such minor matters as arranging the fixtures and checking availability – that was still left to me. The new captain seemed to think that his main duty was to hand out gratuitous advice to both team-mates and opponents alike.

'Sorry, skipper,' I said, attempting to mollify him, 'we were due for a good result and if the trumps behave I . . . '

'You've been due for a good result all evening,' interrupted the club expert, 'and the bad trump break didn't make a scrap of difference. The slam's lay-down.'

This was the hand in question.

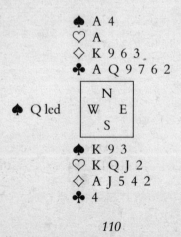

```
              ♠ A 4
              ♡ A
              ◇ K 9 6 3
              ♣ A Q 9 7 6 2
                   ┌─────┐
                   │  N  │
♠ Q led        W   │     │   E
                   │  S  │
                   └─────┘
              ♠ K 9 3
              ♡ K Q J 2
              ◇ A J 5 4 2
              ♣ 4
```

With the South hand I had toiled to 6 ◇ and received the lead of the ♠ Q. I won in dummy and led a low diamond on which East showed out, discarding a low heart. How should the hand be played?

Solution

Declarer wins the opening lead in dummy and leads a low diamond, discovering the bad trump break. He wins with the ◇ A and at trick 3 should lead a further diamond forcing West to split his honours. Declarer wins in dummy, plays a spade to hand and ruffs his losing spade in dummy. He should now cash the ♡ A and the ♣ A before exiting with dummy's ◇ 9. Whatever West returns, the declarer is able to win in hand and draw the outstanding trump. If he makes the mistake of failing to cash the two aces, he can be locked on the table and forced to concede a trump promotion when West holds a singleton club.

Complete deal

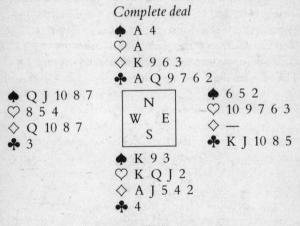

♠ A 4
♡ A
◇ K 9 6 3
♣ A Q 9 7 6 2

♠ Q J 10 8 7
♡ 8 5 4
◇ Q 10 8 7
♣ 3

N
W E
S

♠ 6 5 2
♡ 10 9 7 6 3
◇ —
♣ K J 10 8 5

♠ K 9 3
♡ K Q J 2
◇ A J 5 4 2
♣ 4

Post-mortem

'At any rate, it's a flat board,' I said. 'I suppose the declarer made the same mistake as me?'

'He was never tested,' said the club expert. 'He was

down before he got that far. In fact there was a most peculiar affair at our table. The play to the first three tricks was exactly the same as at yours. It was when the declarer led a spade from dummy at trick 4 that the incident occurred.'

'Incident? What incident?'

'Well, you know how dark it is in the corner where I was sitting?' explained the club expert. 'By mistake I had sorted the ♣ K among my spades and played it, fondly imagining it to be the ♠ K. The error was discovered immediately so there was no question of a revoke, but it did mean that the ♣ K was a penalty card. The opponents thought it was hilarious. With enough tricks for his contract without the spade ruff, the declarer was naturally anxious to get rid of trumps as quickly as possible so he led a diamond towards dummy. My partner stepped in smartly with the ◇ Q and punched dummy with another spade. The declarer now found himself locked on the table with no safe way back to hand to draw the last trump. He suffered the same fate as befell you and was obliged to lose the slam to a trump promotion. Most unfortunate for him. You should have seen his face. It was a picture. He looked just like a man who has bet on red when black turns up.

'As you know, the team captain should always set a good example to others and I apologized profusely for my part in the declarer's downfall. The opponents were most understanding. In fact they're an extremely pleasant bunch and it was a most enjoyable match. Incidentally, there is one other small matter I feel I ought to mention.'

I looked at him suspiciously. 'Well?' I said.

'It's our home match and I believe the captain is responsible for settling the account. Unfortunately, I seem to have mislaid my cheque-book. Would you be kind enough, my dear fellow, to attend to this minor consideration?'

36

Treble Chance

The club expert was not particularly renowned for his friendly disposition so I was quite surprised when he greeted me warmly early one Thursday afternoon in the ante-room of the bridge club.

'My dear chap, what a pleasure to see you. I've been waiting to catch you alone.'

He came over to the small table where I was sitting.

'You may not be aware,' he went on, 'that I am con-ducting a survey into the incidence of "blind spots" among card players of varying degrees of skill. I have canvassed several of the better players in this club on one particular hand with predictable results, and I would value most highly the opinions of others such as yourself.'

'I'm afraid I'm rather busy,' I said, cut to the quick. 'I haven't finished my football coupon yet.'

He glanced down at the table and picked up my client's copy. 'This won't take a moment, I assure you,' he said, 'and after all it is in the interests of science. Ah! Such serendipity. I see you favour the Treble Chance.'

Taking a fountain pen from his waistcoat pocket he wrote down the following hand alongside my column of crosses:

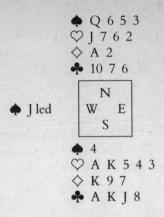

♠ Q 6 5 3
♡ J 7 6 2
◇ A 2
♣ 10 7 6

N
W   E
S

♠ J led

♠ 4
♡ A K 5 4 3
◇ K 9 7
♣ A K J 8

'This deal occurred a few weeks ago in rubber bridge,'
he continued. 'I was playing in a contract of 4 ♡ and
received the lead of the ♠ J. I played low from dummy and
East produced the ♠ 7. West seemed somewhat reluctant
to continue the suit but eventually led the ♠ 10 upon which
East's ♠ K appeared. I ruffed in hand and laid down the
♡ A. West showed out discarding a low diamond. I
crossed to dummy with the ◇ A and led a further spade,
ruffing in my own hand. East's ♠ A appeared on this trick
making dummy's ♠ Q good. I then cashed the ♣ A and
followed up with the ◇ K and ◇ 9 which I ruffed in
dummy. Both opponents followed and the position now
is:

♠ Q
♡ J 7
♢ —
♣ 10 7

```
    N
  W   E
    S
```

♠ —
♡ K 5
♢ —
♣ K J 8

'The lead is on the table and I need three further tricks to make the contract. How should I play?'

Solution

'Well,' asked the club expert, 'have you decided yet?'

'There seem to be two possible lines of play,' I replied. 'You can either take a straightforward club finesse or play dummy's winning spade. The second alternative is best since it gives East the chance to go wrong. If he fails to ruff you make the contract. Even if he does ruff you are no worse off. He has to lead a club himself, or give you a ruff and discard, and you can take the finesse then.'

'And that's your answer?'

'Certainly.'

The club expert nodded wisely. 'Excellent,' he said, making an entry in a small black notebook.

'There wasn't much to that problem,' I said. 'You seem satisfied with my answer.'

'It was certainly the one I expected,' he replied, 'which is always gratifying. However, you made the common error of playing the cards you can see rather than the unseen ones that can be counted. I gave you a clue, you know, when I mentioned Treble Chance. The third line of play is to cash the ♣ A and exit with a low club. If East wins he is end-played since he is down to ♡ Q109. If West wins, East is end-played on the next trick as he is forced to trump West's next lead. The play may be termed, in football parlance, a banker. Speaking of which, I note from your coupon that Chelsea have been selected to draw. Are you sure that this is a wise move? After all, my dear fellow, they *are* playing at Stamford Bridge.'

Complete deal

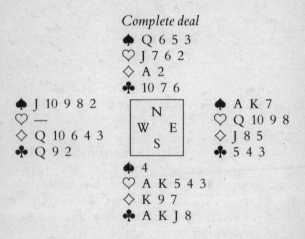

```
                    ♠ Q 6 5 3
                    ♡ J 7 6 2
                    ♢ A 2
                    ♣ 10 7 6
♠ J 10 9 8 2          ┌───────┐          ♠ A K 7
♡ —                   │   N   │          ♡ Q 10 9 8
♢ Q 10 6 4 3          │ W   E │          ♢ J 8 5
♣ Q 9 2               │   S   │          ♣ 5 4 3
                      └───────┘
                    ♠ 4
                    ♡ A K 5 4 3
                    ♢ K 9 7
                    ♣ A K J 8
```